"Don't forget the dill pickles. . . ."

Maggie looked up from her cookfire. Johnny was back from who knew where? Hastings's camp? Annabelle's lair?

He threw an armload of sagebrush near the fire and squatted next to Maggie, one hand held behind his back. "Hastings gives a good talk. Almost good enough to put me off of Oregon. Certainly good enough to confuse many."

"More chin-high clover in California, Johnny?" she couldn't resist asking, though they hadn't been doing much talking lately.

"Maybe. But nothing like this." He pulled the hand from behind his back and presented his wife with a yellow cactus flower. It was frail, yet lovely, the fleeting, unexpected blossom of the desert.

She put out her hand to accept the offering, a small smile forming on her face, then pulled back. "It would go better with the widow's black hair, wouldn't it?"

Johnny growled in frustration and threw the flower in the fire. They both watched it shrivel into ashes. He got up.

"I'm not sure what it is you're wanting from me, Meg. But I'm beginning to believe that, whatever it is, I can't be giving it."

KATHLEEN KARR is the author of several romance novels, including the best-selling *From This Day Forward*, which won the "Gold Medallion" Award for romance fiction.

Books by Kathleen Karr

HEARTSONG PRESENTS

HP23—Gone West
  (Destiny's Dreamers / Book One)

Destiny's Dreamers / Book Two

The
Promised Land

Kathleen Karr

Heartsong Presents

For Anne Severance

ISBN 1-55748-405-8

THE PROMISED LAND

PRINTED IN U.S.A.

cast of characters

Maggie Stuart: Maggie is now twenty, the mother of baby Charlotte and seven-year-old adopted Jamie. Maggie's fire-red hair and blue eyes disguise a nature quick to protect the underdog and vastly protective of those she includes in her extended family. Maggie is bright and always willing to learn from the experiences of others, no matter who those others may be. Filled with faith and optimism, she believes strongly enough in God and in herself to overcome any obstacle, as she overcame her brief capture by Pawnee chief Red Eagle at the conclusion of *Destiny's Dreamers, Book 1: Gone West.*

Johnny Stuart: Johnny is twenty-three and takes his responsibilities as head of family seriously. There is still a touch of the dreamer in this tall, curly black-haired man. He wants above all to take his printing press and words to the new frontier, but Maggie and his children are essential to him in this endeavor. His unarmed, single-handed rescue of his wife from the Pawnee was the result of intelligence, desperation, and newfound skills as a man of action as well as words.

Irish and Gwen Hardisty: A charming, excitable young potter and his attractive, older sister, a seamstress.

Sam Thayer: A brawny, tongue-tied blacksmith and suitor to Gwen Hardisty.

Max and Hazel Kreller: Emigrants from Pennsylvania who, with their three daughters, become staunch friends of the Stuarts.

Joshua Chandler: Elected captain of the wagon train.

Grandma Richman: A strong woman with healing skills who is shepherding her eight grandchildren West after the accidental death of her ne'er-do-well son on the trail.

5

Reverend Josiah Winslow: A stern man with private reasons for heading West—and for keeping his family isolated from the rest of the Chandler Party.

Red Eagle: Chief of a Pawnee tribe of the plains, husband to Corn Girl and Evening Star, and abductor of Maggie—his choice for a third wife.

Snake: Enemy to Red Eagle, slain in mortal combat by Johnny Stuart.

spring, 1846
The Oregon Trail

Johnny and Maggie Stuart and their young family are en route to the Oregon Territory. Unlike other emigrants seeking land, the Stuarts carry with them books and a printing press to bring the written Word of God and man to new lands.

In *Destiny's Dreamers, Book 1: Gone West,* the Stuarts embarked from Independence, Missouri, with the Chandler Party, a train of thirty wagons of emigrants. The early journey was unusually wet and treacherous, causing the Stuarts to form close cooperative bonds with the Hardistys and Sam Thayer, offering home-cooked meals in return for future help. The potential of marauding Indians also upset the train, resulting in a few stolen horses, one death, and Maggie's abduction.

The conclusion to the Stuarts' epic journey begins after Maggie has been freed by Johnny from her brief captivity among the Pawnee. The Chandler Party has covered four hundred miles of the two-thousand-mile trek to their promised land.

one

Several miles from the Pawnee village Maggie and Johnny came upon their relief party. The band of a dozen men from the wagon train were hot, tired, dusty, and frustrated. Their horses looked worse. Johnny reined in.

"I see you've got her back again," Chandler commented, wiping a ring of dust from the neck beneath his great beard.

"What happened, Johnny?" Irish was pent-up excitement. "You're bleeding!"

Johnny swiped a hand at his forgotten wound. "It's a long story. I kind of figured you'd be trailing a little closer, once I realized you'd chase after us one way or the other."

"Took a wrong turn. Got lost." Sam was disgusted. He spat the travel grit from his mouth and they all watched the moisture curl into a dustball on the prairie.

The horses fretted. They were as uncomfortable as the two parties, both fearful of hearing what had actually transpired.

"Are the children all right, Max?"

Max inspected Maggie's beaded buckskin with interest. "Hazel will have everything under control. We haven't been back since before dawn ourselves. Fine rescue posse *we* turned out to be."

"We've all had a bad night, Max. But I'm fine." Maggie raised her voice so all the party might hear. "Thank you for your thoughtfulness, all of you. Johnny made it—just

7

in time." They would never know just how narrow her escape had been. Her eyes gleamed at her husband.

Johnny felt suddenly shy. He felt something else, too. It was a need to be absolutely alone with his wife for a little longer. "Can you find your way back? If you can, I'd appreciate it if you'd spread the word we're on our way. My wife's had a rough time of it, and I'd like to go easier—" His words were placating, but his eyes issued a direct order. *Head on back, and leave us alone!*

Sam picked up the message loud and clear. He nudged his horse. "Guess the women are gonna be plumb distraught, all this time with no word. What do you say, Chandler? Maybe we can get a shot at one of them deer we left unmolested on the way over. It'd make us a nice feast tonight. A proper homecoming feast."

Chandler grunted something into his beard and tipped his hat at Maggie. "Pleased to have you back safe and sound, Missus Stuart. I trust you've gotten the wandering yen outta your system."

Maggie blushed through the sunburn on her face. "Indeed, I have, Mr. Chandler. It will not occur again."

"I'll see to it that it don't! I'm gonna double the sentries and read the women and children their rights and duties." Chandler kicked his horse and led the posse back toward the Platte.

Johnny sat astride his horse, studying Maggie, but saying nothing. Neither had spoken since they'd left the village. At first, it was in the sheer relief of escape, but now Maggie could feel the silence building into something else, something different. She returned her husband's steady gaze.

"We'd better put more distance between us and the

Pawnee." Evading the subject of their unspoken conflict, Johnny led them into motion again.

By late afternoon they could see the line of the Platte shimmering brightly like some mirage in the distance before them. They could also make out the bluff near their camp. The wagons would be beyond. Johnny reined in next to a small stream that was struggling to meet the same river they were bound for.

"The horses need a drink and a rest." He slid from the stallion and began to lead it to the water.

Maggie tried the same. Suddenly she felt weak, felt herself faltering. "Johnny!"

He looked up, then came running to help.

She stood in his arms as the horses made for their drink. "Forgive me, Johnny . . . please forgive me for everything. I'm so tired—"

His arms held her, but there was little strength in them. They tightened marginally. "It's I who should be asking for forgiveness . . . after the ordeal you've had this last day and night."

"We've got to talk, Johnny. Without the others around us. Can't we steal another few moments here . . . alone?"

Johnny led her to a clean piece of stream upcurrent from the animals. He eased her down next to it gently, but his movements were stiff, almost foreign. He stood staring at his wife while he unwound the bandanna around his neck, ignoring the blood that had thickened on it. Carefully rinsing it in the stream, he brought the cloth to her face and dabbed the cool liquid over her eyes, her nose, her throat.

"What's the matter, Johnny? Why are you so distant? Have I changed that much in a night and a day?"

"Your clothing is certainly different."

Maggie glanced down at the forgotten buckskins. "It was Corn Girl's best outfit. Now she'll have to make herself another."

Johnny was not listening. "All duded up for a wedding. *My wife*. Prepared to take another man."

"Johnny! There was no choice! How could you think I would willingly—"

"Why did you go to the spring last night, Meg? In your nightclothes! Even Winslow took notice of your escapade!"

"Winslow has been spying on every decent female in the train since we left Kansas, and well you know it."

"It's not Winslow I'm talking about, but you. Not any other woman in the train, just you, my wife!"

"It was hot, and I only meant to cool myself a little. Besides . . . I missed you, Johnny."

"Is that sufficient reason to break security, to violate the bonds of convention?"

"I wasn't thinking about any of that. And how was I to know that Red Eagle hadn't given up, that he was anywhere about?"

"You should have known! Were I Red Eagle, I would never give you up! I've been chastising myself all through the long search for you, wondering where I'd gone wrong—"

"But, Johnny, you haven't gone wrong! You're still my husband, my only husband. I still love you more than the world itself!"

He raised damp hands to his hair, shoving his fingers through the tangled coal-black curls in frustration. "It's not enough. Can't you understand? You must *know*, know what you're capable of doing to a man!"

"But I don't want to *do* anything to any man but you!" It came out as a wail. They were arguing in circles. They were fighting about something that Maggie was only beginning to grasp. They were actually *fighting*, for the first time. And so soon after she had been saved.

Johnny's voice rose, too. "I killed a man today— because of you! He may have been an Indian, and an evil one at that, but he was still a man—a human being. I offered to kill another one. A better man. For you, Meg. For you!" He shook his head despairingly, adding softly, "I never thought I would bring death to a living soul. I hoped only to be the bearer of light, of knowledge! Doesn't that give you some idea of your power?"

Maggie reached out a hand to touch him, to comfort him. He was hurting, too. "Not of my power, but the strength of our love. You were magnificent, Johnny . . . and frightening. You were all control and energy, all righteous indignation. Elemental. I'll never forget the look in your eyes when you entered the lodge to find me. To challenge Snake. There was a righteous anger burning in your eyes—"

He shrugged off her gesture. He wasn't listening. This woman with hair like the setting sun and eyes like lightning. Did he really know her at all? Had he ever known her? He reached out for her and drew her impulsively into his arms.

She could feel a new wetness. It was his tears streaming down. Suddenly she was no longer afraid of this man. Her arms went out to enfold her husband against her, to love him.

Maggie bestowed healing kisses on the long gash in

Johnny's neck, on other wounds yet unspoken of in his defending arms. He would carry scars till the end of his days to remind him of this particular day. Maggie would, too. But her scars would be carried more silently, within.

They returned to their horses in silence. It was a different kind of silence—the silence of rekindled peace, the silence of love and understanding. There would be time for words later.

The campsite awaiting them held a festive air. Deer were roasting at the spit. Clean laundry waved like welcoming flags from the white-tops. Men, women, and children were tending their tasks with energy and smiles. It was a different vision from that which had greeted Maggie so many worlds away at the Indian village that morning, but she could not help being struck by the sameness of it. A crowd gathered around the two on horseback, greeting them like returning conquerors. But Maggie's mind switched back to realities quickly. She was no heroine. She only wanted to see her children.

Helping hands brought her gently down from the horse, then Jamie was hurtling himself into her buckskin skirts, and Hazel was coming into view, arms filled with Maggie's own baby. Visions of Corn Girl's empty cradleboard came, unbidden, to Maggie's mind. Tears stung her eyes as she knelt to hug Jamie, to reach for her daughter, to thank God for her deliverance.

"Where'd you get the clothes?"

"Are you all right?"

"What did they do to you?"

"Did those savages . . . did they meddle with you?"

Maggie stared through blurred eyes at the questioners

around her. She was news. She was excitement coming into their closed daily existence. The women surrounded her like so many buzzards picking at the bones of a bloodied carcass. She couldn't handle them. Not now. Not yet.

Maggie stood up. She was vastly encumbered by her two clinging children, but gloried in the encumbrance.

"I'm sorry. I'm not quite ready . . . I'll answer your questions when I'm more able, I promise. Red Eagle and his wives were courteous and . . . yes, *civilized*. Johnny can tell you more."

But Johnny was not about to tell anyone more. He gathered together his family and herded them to their own campsite, where a joint of meat had been left cooking for them. Trying to find some semblance of privacy, he finally led them all into the hot closeness of the caravan and shut the door.

He leaned against it, wiping sweat from his brow. "Thank God. We made it through the press."

Maggie gave him a worried look. "You've broken open your wounds, Johnny. Let me tend to them."

"No. Care for the baby first."

Maggie shook a leg in an effort to extricate Jamie and Bacon. Both boy and coyote pup were entangled underfoot. "At least, take a pan and boil some water. When it's ready, we'll clean the cuts properly."

"You really want me to go back out there again?"

Maggie smiled. "It's not the Pawnee waiting, Johnny. It's our own people."

"At this point I'm unsure which is worse."

They laughed together, shared a hug, and made the moves necessary to return life to normal.

Over the next several days Maggie shared her story slowly with Gwen and Hazel and Grandma Richman. With Gwen, who was growing into love with Sam, she shared the most—her ambivalence about Red Eagle, his poetry, the kindnesses of Corn Girl and Evening Star. Most especially she tried to express Johnny's transformation from a man of dreams into a man of action.

Gwen swallowed her stories piecemeal and digested them with relish. "Heavens, Maggie, being courted by an Indian chief!"

"Unwashed, Gwen, remember that. Unwashed."

"It couldn't be worse than some of the men around here. Take Al Jarboe. I'll bet he hasn't been out of his longjohns since stepping into them last autumn."

Maggie wrinkled her nose. "His wife can take him, although how she does evades me."

Gwen glossed over Maggie's distaste, still concentrating on Red Eagle. "All those feathers woven into his hair. I wonder if he takes them out before bed?"

"I really haven't the faintest idea, Gwen. And why this sudden interest? I was under the impression that most men frightened you."

"They still do. Except for Sam. He's not most men, after all, although he doesn't know it yet." Gwen sighed from the heart. "It's the romance of it, Maggie. Like those novels written by Mr. Cooper. Johnny is just like Natty Bumpo, saving you from the Indians. And your Corn Girl is a little like Dew-of-June. Then there's the chieftain Chingachgook—"

Maggie almost lost her temper. "This is not fiction, Gwen. Not Cooper or Scott! And I assure you there was little romance about Red Eagle's dusty village. It nearly brought out the missionary in me. A few more days and I would have bit the bullet and started bathing the dirty children, and given instructions on irrigation!"

"You wouldn't!"

"Why not? Better I should adopt Indian ways?"

Gwen considered. "And what would you have done about Red Eagle's advances?"

"I assure you, when the time came, I would have had no choice on that account."

She noted Gwen's quiver of excitement and sighed to herself. Here was a woman who refused to be touched. Yet, inside, she was yearning to be loved. Is this what happened to all spinsters? No wonder there was money to be made in the ladies' romances Johnny refused to burden their caravan with. And how would Gwen have taken to Snake's particular style of advance?

Maggie had purposely neglected to mention that incident—at least the precise details of it. Johnny had merely found her struggling with the angry brave. That was part of what Johnny had been confused about. Trying to deal with the something in her, Maggie, the something that had brought about Snake's attack. They hadn't worked it all out yet. They probably wouldn't for many long nights to come.

"Red Eagle's advances were completely verbal, Gwen, and only verbal. The man never laid a hand on me, except to drag me by the hair through the prairie grass."

"It must've been some dragging. You've got them covered up now, but I spied your bruises when you were washing up this morning behind the wagon. You're all over black and blue! How you managed to start right in again droving the oxen, I'll never know."

"One does what one must." Maggie's fingers, never idle, were skinning another of Sam's jackrabbits. Her extended family had begun to develop a taste for them. A lot like chicken they were, though there were some on the train who'd starve rather than consume *vermin* of this sort.

"Nevertheless—"

"Nevertheless, nothing. Take this skin and peg it the way I showed you, Gwen."

Gwen tentatively reached for the messy fur with two fingertips. "Is this really necessary, Maggie?"

"Yes, it is. Waste not, want not. Do a good job with the cleaning, and I'll teach you how to stitch together a fine pair of mittens for Sam, come cold weather."

Gwen brightened, still holding the offending skin a good distance from her body. "You won't need to give me any lessons in tailoring, Maggie. I guess I know enough about that!"

"Excuse me. I keep forgetting—"

"Yes, I do hold some form of competence. Not that anyone has noticed recently from my cooking." Gwen smiled wryly.

Maggie had to laugh. "We're all given different gifts, Gwen."

"It seems to me sometimes that the Lord parcels them out unevenly." Rabbit skin outstretched before her, Gwen disappeared from the campfire, muttering about the ridiculousness of preparing for winter in the dog days of summer.

Maggie shook her head as she watched her friend go. Even after all this time on the trail, Gwen was still a city girl. She had trouble understanding the most basic things that a farm-bred child was raised to know without thinking—most important of which was that one prepared for the lean times during the bounteous ones.

Maggie drew her attention back to the supper. Not that this was a completely bounteous time. If only they'd spy buffalo soon. Their tiny cabin was becoming easier and easier to walk through as the supplies of grains melted away. It didn't seem right that her family might have to face real hunger soon, and it not even winter. She stopped stock still a moment, considering. What day was it? What month? It felt as if they'd been on the journey for years, for always.

Johnny returned to the circle of wagons, bouncing Charlotte on his back. Jamie followed with arms full of buffalo chips.

"Do you know the day, Johnny?"

The question stopped him. "Monday? Tuesday?"

"No, I mean what day and month."

"Let me check." He went over to his white-top and hovered next to the scratches he'd been making with his knife on the sideboard each morning. "Jamie! Come here. I've got a sum for you to do."

Jamie dropped his load, raced over, and began counting the marks. The sum completed, the two put their heads together, as if deliberating on a most serious issue. Finally they nodded solemnly and turned.

Johnny cleared his throat. "After due consideration, Jamie and I have reached a scientific conclusion. It is—"

"June fourth!" shouted Jamie.

Maggie ran a handkerchief over her damp face. "It's not even proper summer yet. What will these plains be like in another month or two?"

"Hellish," threw in Sam as he joined them, shirtsleeves rolled up to his biceps, buttons peeled open to reveal the furry mat covering his chest. He squatted morosely just out of the fire's perimeter of heat.

Johnny and the children took off after another load of fuel. Gwen was still struggling with the little rabbit skin.

Maggie gave the big man a hard look. "What's the matter?"

"Gwen." Then, in a burst of eloquence, "What does it take to convince a woman you love her?"

"Maybe saving her from wild Indians," smiled Maggie, trying to make light of her too-recent encounter.

Sam shuddered. "We can thank God the Pawnee stopped shadowing us. Not a sight of another soul save us these three days." His shaggy brows furrowed again. "Know I'm not much for looks, Maggie. But I'm strong and willing, and everything I have I've offered to the woman. I even suggested Winslow might tie us up, he bein' a parson an' all." A ghost of a smile crossed under his mustache. "Guess that were the wrong approach. She don't look on him as a man of God a'tall."

Maggie considered Sam's dilemma. "We're coming onto Fort Laramie soon, Sam. There's bound to be another preacher there. Or maybe a man of the law. That would make it legal. Perhaps even the proctor of the fort. Isn't he like the captain of a ship? Give her a little more time. Pressure confuses her."

"If she be confused, what of me? Never did meet any other I wanted." His eyes were soulful with the image of the woman he loved before them. "She's so delicate, so needful of protection. I'd cherish her, I would." He stopped. "It's all or nothing, Maggie!"

Maggie turned the spit, smiling broadly now that her back was to Sam. The bounties of Gwen's hour-glass figure had never struck her as delicate. But next to Sam's hugeness, perhaps they were. Beauty was, after all, in the eye of the beholder. "You'll have it all soon, Sam. Be patient."

At that moment, the subject of their discussion walked into view, wiping soiled fingers on her skirts with a look of disgust. Maggie watched the two shy lovers as they spied each other, both reddening, Gwen hiding her scuffed hands behind her back.

"Why don't you two take a stroll. I've got things under control here, and it's certain to be cooler down by the riverbank."

Sam sprang up with alacrity, his moroseness gone. They ambled off together. Sam's arm offered support and, after a moment's consideration on Gwen's part, was tentatively accepted. Maggie smiled again.

Two days later, the supper cooking, Maggie walked carefully into the surrounding prairie to hunt for early berries and the odd chicory root. Hearing a rustling in the grass beyond, she stopped stock still. Not more Indians. *Please, Lord, anything but more Indians.*

She lowered herself carefully to her knees and parted the grasses before her without a sound. Her breath returned. It was not Indians.

Not more than ten yards away, Sam and Gwen sat on the grasses facing each other, a proper two feet of space between them. They were engrossed in their conversation, Maggie's nearness unknown to them. As she gathered her skirts to retreat, Maggie suddenly put a hand to her throat. There was a snake, a large snake, only inches from Gwen's back.

She opened her mouth to give warning, but Sam's sharp eyes had caught the reptile's movement. In a gesture remarkable for its speed, his hand shot out and grasped the snake behind the neck. Ignoring the still seeking fangs, Sam broke the neck with a sure, sharply cracking twist. Only then did he pull up the remainder of the pyramided body. A rattle was revealed at the end of the impressive tail.

Gwen turned pale. Crying out, she threw herself into Sam's waiting arms. Grinning, he cast the rattler aside and welcomed the woman of his dreams into his embrace.

Maggie disappeared discreetly, wishing only that such a moment could be hers, with Johnny.

two

A week short of Fort Laramie, the train spotted a dark mass in the distance, low on the horizon. It was too low for storm clouds, and too big for elk. Buffalo were before them at last. Haste was made to set up camp, though it was only mid-afternoon. Amid much excitement, the men departed for the hunt.

Johnny rode with his friends, feeling suddenly more alive than he had since Meg's rescue. What was this newness that was overtaking him? This surge of blood coursing through his veins at the thought of possible danger? His years as a bookish peddler seemed part of another life. The daily drudgery of traveling across the plains was forgotten. The hunt became all, and he welcomed the challenge as he would have welcomed fresh rains from the sky. Johnny let Dickens have his head.

It was finally Max who caught up with him, motioning him to slow down. "No hurry, Stuart. Wouldn't want to stampede them, eh?"

Johnny made an effort to rein in both the horse and himself. "Sorry. It must've been the moment, Max."

"The Pawnee changed you some, Johnny. Not to worry though. There's lots of excitement ahead."

Johnny felt chagrin. He let his friend ease off to the side. Was his need that evident? Would that one day's encounter leave him restless for life, as restless for adventure as he once had been for new places and sights?

He rolled his head and straightened his back. What of

it? The reasons could be dealt with later. The buffalo were close now. Their great bodies were sending off heat and odors to further incite Johnny and the horse upon which he sat. Johnny pulled his rifle from its sidemount, spurred Dickens once more, and went in for the kill.

He didn't stop to count the wild herd before him, but drove relentlessly into the midst of a hundredfold or more of great lowing monsters. A kind of madness had overtaken him, and he heeded neither the shoves of vast maned bodies nor the butt of horns.

Johnny whooped aloud. "This is seeing the elephant, boys!"

He pulled his trigger and the first shot rang out. The dumb beasts, having generally ignored Johnny's entry into their party, looked up with surprise. They began to move away. At first, they moved slowly. Then with a lumbering strength and stolidity, they began to run. Johnny's gun had been prepared, and he shot again, hitting yet another cow. He waited to see the effects of his shots. They had been true.

The first cow gave Johnny a long glance full of disbelief and betrayal. She lay herself gently down, curled her tail, coughed up blood, and was still. The second—equally disbelieving—fell to her knees. Making a final effort she rose again, as if to run. Finally she, too, released her life's blood.

Johnny's mouth had been open for one of his Highland war whoops. But something in the eyes of these animals stopped him. His stomach lurched, and he knew he was about to be sick. This was not like Snake, whom he had engaged in hand-to-hand combat. Not like one man pitting his wits and strengths against another, to the death, for a cause. Not at all like that. This was sheer, outright slaughter. The meat was necessary, but he'd never thought to receive a look like that from a buffalo. Wishing he'd remained on the rim of the herd, like the others—on the edge looking in, innocent of those final stares—Johnny swallowed his bile.

It was Sam's shout that roused him. "Stuart! Behind you! The bull!"

Johnny spun round. A furious bull thundered down on him, trying too late to protect his harem. Eyes filled with murder, nose and mouth spuming froth, the great horned head let out a bellow and lowered itself, Johnny fixed in its sights.

He raised his rifle and took aim. Too late he remembered it was empty. He kicked Dickens viciously, but the horse had not been bred for quick reflexes. The bull closed in.

Johnny searched madly for a route of escape. In the midst of moving bodies, there was none. Without thought, he dropped the rifle, loosed his boots from the stirrups, spun around the saddle, and vaulted onto the head of the bull. The shock of his assault stunned the animal. It halted its mindless drive just short of Dickens.

Hanging on for dear life, with one hand on a horn, Johnny reversed himself on the animal's back. He pulled out his hunting knife and stabbed between a rib. It was as if his knife had been a mosquito. The bull twitched its heavily matted fur and bucked its hind legs to rid himself of the larger annoyance seated there. Johnny struck again and again. Finally, in desperation, he leaned over the bull's side and struck for the heart. The last blow went home. The bull gave a last, heartrending bellow of outrage and fell near his cows.

Johnny remained glued to the animal's back. It was Max who finally pulled his stallion within a safe distance of the dying bull. Tentatively moving in, he reached up over the huge bulk, and one by one released Johnny's frozen fingers from their grip.

Max spoke softly into the ebbing din of battle. "Got it all out of your system now, Johnny? I hope so. I wasn't looking forward to carrying your body back to Maggie. She'd have had a hard time understanding."

Johnny's eyes focused slowly on Max and his words. "It is enough. 'There are few die well that die in a battle.' "

"Not sure who you're quoting, but the words are right fair. Put your mind back to your books, Johnny. It's what you were made for."

Johnny slid down the hot, mountainous back. "Shakespeare. It may be you're right, Max. Still, there's that in me fighting it. Fighting it hard. My father was a man of words and peace—an old man already at my birth—but the line he came from was not. Rock hard his people were. Craggy as the hills of Scotland. And some called my grandfather by the name of Bonnie Prince Charlie."

Max shook his head. "I'm a simple man. Those wars were before my time. Look to the future, Johnny, not the past."

Johnny shook his head and tested his legs for landworthiness. "I'm trying."

The rest of the hunting party arrived, eyes filled with awe and not a little frightened respect. Slowly they dismounted to take in Johnny and his catch.

"You single-handedly doubled our take, Stuart."

Chandler scratched his head. "Not sure I approve of your methods, though."

Johnny stood up straight and made one of the bows he'd always saved for his book sales—lithe and elegant, suggesting amused subservience. "John Stuart, at your service. Please accept my buffalo . . . and my apologies for a somewhat unusual hunting style. I'll make every effort not to let it happen again."

Chandler spat and smiled. "Guess I don't really care how you bagged 'em. Iffen you can keep yourself alive in the process, you got my blessing to take on the chore for all of us next hunt. We'll jest save ourselves the ride out an' back."

To the roar of the other men, the cleaning began. Buffalo ribs were propped up before a crackling blaze. Maggie was stuffing cleaned intestines with prime tidbits of tenderloin mixed with fat, chopped liver, and spices. Earlier sausages sputtered enthusiastically on sticks within the fire.

Irish, no longer able to wait, pulled his out and bit into it. He sighed with pleasure. "My hat is off to you, Maggie, me girl. If this be haggis, and your Johnny a reborn Highlander, there's something to be said for Scotland that my Irish parents never passed on to me."

Maggie smiled, but she was troubled. The men had been regaling her with tales of the hunt. Johnny was once more the hero of the day. But at what cost? What cost, indeed?

Jamie interrupted her thoughts. "Tell me again about my pa's tricks, Uncle Irish. Why couldn't I have been there to see them? I would've traded nearly anything for it."

Irish threw a bite to the coyote pup at his feet. "You would've traded off Bacon here for the pleasure?"

That almost stumped Jamie, but he slowly nodded his head. "Yup. I would have!"

"Don't go putting ideas into the boy's head, Irish," Johnny spoke up. "He'd never part with that animal."

"I would, too. Well, for a few minutes, at least. That's 'cause I know Bacon wouldn't stay with anyone else. He'd come running right back home to me."

They had to laugh at the boy's satisfied logic.

"It was the nearest thing I ever seen to a circus," threw in Sam. "Mighty impressive acrobatics. Had my heart in my mouth."

"Not too far in," commented Johnny dryly. "You had enough room to spit out a warning that saved both Dickens and me."

Gwen beamed at Sam proudly. Instead of blushing, Sam took her hand and clasped it in his big paw. She did not trouble to remove it.

"The main thing was the quick thinking," said Irish between bites. "I never saw anybody react that way. It made me think I'd follow Johnny into battle without a doubt."

Maggie watched her husband as a cloud crossed his face. It was the fighting business again, this new realization of his hidden strengths, his *manhood*. Hadn't he realized his own true self yet, as he had tried to make her aware of her own hidden nature? Had he not come to the understanding that violence did not make the man? She was constantly intrigued by his new ways. Occasionally she was excited by them. Yet she longed passionately for the sound stability of their past together. Maggie wouldn't hamper him, but she *was* going to Oregon for him. She wanted him there with her when she arrived.

Johnny bent down, hiding the look in his eyes as he prodded the ribs. "I pronounce these ready to consume."

"If that means eat, pass 'em out, afore *I* pass out from starvation!"

Gwen smiled fondly at Sam's words. "An event unlikely to happen anytime soon. Not while your bones hold on to that brawn!"

Sam flexed his biceps for his sweetheart's benefit. They all laughed and dug in.

More meat had been caught than the entire train could eat in one night of frenzied gorging. The following day had to be set aside for the preserving of what was left. Campfires smoked strongly next to almost every wagon. The travelers began to learn and accept the lessons of the Indians and mountain men before them.

Maggie, with her husband's assistance, was further occupied in cleaning the skin of the huge old bull he'd single-handedly killed. Johnny had given the other skins to Max and Sam for their part in the affair. As Maggie scraped, she couldn't help noticing the knife rents in the skin. She fingered each of them speculatively, her mind filled with images of Johnny inflicting the wounds.

She hadn't been present at this particular exhibition of his newfound skills—or was it madness? But she had witnessed his conquest of Snake. Johnny hadn't spoken of yesterday's incident yet, and she was waiting for him to unburden himself.

Doubt crossed her mind as they worked silently on opposite sides of the skin. Would he speak, or continue to ignore this episode, another little piece of himself unshared with her? She fervently prayed for his voice, for his willingness to bring her back to him where she belonged.

"Do you think I should stitch these holes together when the skin is ready?" she prodded.

"What? Oh. If it pleases you. It would be sort of like stitching the history out of the thing, though."

"I hadn't thought of it that way, Johnny. I was only thinking of the skin in terms of a blanket. A very warm one like the Indians use. It seemed as if the holes would let in cold air."

He continued scraping with a preoccupied air. "Do as you think best."

"Johnny, I'm asking what *you* think best."

He raised his head to look at her. "I suggested what *I* thought already. If the holes and what they represent do not appeal to you, by all means make them disappear."

"I don't want to make it all disappear, Johnny. It's part of you now, isn't it? I just want to be allowed into your mind and heart so I can understand."

He glanced away, saying nothing.

"Johnny. Don't do this to me. Please. I'm begging, Johnny. This is worse than when you went off each year with your father and I was left to another twelve months on the farm, wondering what new things you would be doing that I would never see, would never understand. Wondering if you'd ever really return to me! It's hard being the one left waiting, Johnny. . . . I know it's mostly a woman's lot, but I thought we had something different together from other men and women, other husbands and wives. We've always shared, Johnny . . . everything."

He stopped his work. "What is it you really want from

me, Meg? My soul? How can I give you what I no longer understand?"

He was in pain. Maggie dropped her tool and reached out to touch his face. "I'm not God, Johnny. And I'm not the devil, either. I'm your wife, the mother of your children. I'm the one human being who cares enough, loves enough, to want to help. Don't push me away."

His own tool fell unheeded from his hand as he grasped hers, rubbing it across his rough cheek. "I've wanted to talk to you, Meg, only God knows how much. But the words, the words that always came so easily are no longer there. Be patient with me a little longer while I try to work it out, try to regain them."

Maggie sighed. "I'll try, Johnny."

"The baby!" Jamie came screeching up, excitement bursting from every pore of his body. "Charley!"

Maggie and Johnny both jumped up.

"What's the matter with her?"

"Did something happen to Charlotte?"

"She's started in to walk!" explained Jamie.

Maggie fell into Johnny's arms, and felt their hearts pounding together. "Dear God," she whispered into his shoulder, "I don't think I can handle any more drama."

Johnny's arms around her tightened, then eased. They followed Jamie. Their red-headed daughter was hanging onto a wagon spoke, standing on wobbly legs, crowing with joy.

three

Laramie.

Maggie built up the fort in her mind as a respite from the worries and fears that had beset her since the Red Eagle incident. She was counting on it to release Johnny's attentions from the abduction and subsequent events. She was praying for a little piece of eastern civilization in the midst of the desolate lands they traveled. Something to remind them of home. Something to bind them together again.

Sam was praying for a binding, too. Gwen had given her word that if a suitable clergyman were present, she would consent to marriage at last. Unbeknownst to Sam, Gwen had been up late nights for the past week. She was using up precious candles stitching together an appropriate wedding dress from a bolt of cloth tucked in her wagon. Sam was not the only one whose heart was set on Fort Laramie.

Irish had thought about Fort Laramie, and thought about Sue Chandler. He'd also thought quite a bit about the proximity of Papa Chandler's shotgun. Truth to tell, he liked what he saw in the girl—a most pleasant piece of clay, but how would it fire? Irish liked to experiment with his materials. No, he wasn't committing himself yet.

Grandma Richman was running out of clothing for her eight charges. Even with her experience, she never would have guessed the trail would have taken such a toll on their britches. Shucks, the soles of their feet were hardened enough for the prairie dust and even the rocks of the Badlands now, but would their shoes fit come cold weather? Even with the food coming and going in fits and spurts like feast or famine, the younguns were still growing. And she hadn't a decent piece of money, either.

Maybe she could trade off something, like that big old cherry dresser they'd been carting so far. Make more room in the wagon, give the stock less to haul, too. But would anyone at the fort want it?

They'd begun passing the droppings of last year's wagons. Some right pretty claw-footed chairs and tables—even carved dressers close on to hers—studded the trail at intervals, all worn by the wind and weather. Her own grandpa had imported that dresser direct from England. It had been her mother's joy. It would hurt. It was hard to leave pieces of yourself behind. But she'd already left her son back in that shallow grave. And no-account that he'd been, there wasn't nothing harder than that.

Hazel Kreller was fixed on the fort, too. Her milk was drying up. She'd thought it was just from the cows slacking off, producing less and less as the way became harder, giving her less to drink. Now she knew the truth. She was pregnant again. Little Irene would have to grow fond of porridge and the remaining squeezings of cow's milk mighty soon. The trouble was the baby was fighting it, and Hazel couldn't blame her. She'd nursed the other girls till they were past two. It was a hard thing, making her ache for the child.

She hadn't told Max yet, either. He'd been busy fussing over his sickening horses, worrying like they were his own flesh and blood. Laramie seemed to be a kind of breaking point in her mind. She saw it as a real town, like the little one in Pennsylvania where they'd come from. Somehow she'd already decorated it with neat houses, green trees, even vegetable patches. They'd walk through the streets, she and Max, hand in hand, like they used to when they were courting. She'd tell him then.

Ruth Winslow was praying hard over Laramie. Her husband had changed since they'd begun this missionary journey. Certainly, the change had started sooner, back in Illinois in that summer of '44. If she'd been a cursing woman, she would have consigned Joseph Smith to the region of hell faster than her husband's assassination plot had. But the damage was long since done—the damage that had made her husband more difficult every blessed day of their lives since Carthage. How he'd cried, actually cried in her arms when he'd come home shaking from that long-ago mission.

He'd confessed the whole thing to her—how he'd helped to plan it, but hadn't actually raised his own arm in violence. It had been the one and only moment of true closeness they'd ever had together. She'd almost thanked God for that blessed moment of sharing, brought on by the Mormons. But it had turned into too little, too late. She'd be paying for that moment for the rest of her life.

She'd always known it was her born duty to follow where the Reverend led, but her husband was making the following harder every day. She was growing thin and old on this trip. It was not vanity which made her notice the fact, may the Lord believe and forgive her. It was a too-soon-from-worrying old.

Ruth knew she shouldn't be attaching herself to earthly things like her sons, but instead put her mind to heaven. Still, she'd be a plain unnatural mother if she could continue to watch her boys grow thinner yet, without concern, while the other wagon children thrived. She'd tried sneaking them her own plates of food. But the Reverend had caught her at it and forbade her to continue. If the Lord wanted them all to get to their mission, He would see that it was so. She'd tried believing. She'd also tried to feed her family what the others ate. The Reverend forbade that, too. Oh, yes, he himself was thriving: slimmer, but rock hard.

He took on less and less work, leaving it for her while he politicked with the men, or spied on the women. She knew he was doing it and had even mentioned the fact. Once. He'd beaten her for her pains, and she hadn't even the comfort of the other women to go to. Like that Maggie Stuart who always gave her such consoling looks, even after her abduction by the heathen. Ruth Winslow shivered. Imagine surviving such a thing. Imagine *wishing* to survive such a thing. She'd have done away with herself. Surely the Lord would forgive that sooner than—

But in Laramie perhaps there'd be another man of God, one she could take her troubles to. One she could talk to about her husband's ever-ballooning fantasies of Mormon revenge, fantasies that even the real threat and dangers of the surrounding Indians had not put from his mind. It would be a solace.

The Reverend Josiah Winslow was possibly the only soul on the Chandler train not looking forward to Laramie. He'd checked out their own train thoroughly for Mormon agents, though he'd almost slipped up way back with that Sam Thayer. Should've known better than to leave footprints behind him like that. But Thayer had been the best and last prospect—the only single man on the trip, strong and resourceful. Those were two traits he'd learn to look for in a Danite.

Now that he was comfortable his own train was clean, here they were coming into new territory, new potential dangers. Brigham Young's agents could easily have dashed ahead of their own plodding wagons. Even now there could be Angels prowling around Laramie, just waiting for the first trains of the season to arrive. Winslow knew *they* knew he was on one of this season's trains. Still, they did not know his exact identity. Maybe he could still play out this game of revenge better than they. If only the train need not stop at Laramie. . . .

four

A violent rain squall broke out as the Chandler Party finally spied Fort Laramie in the distance, the reward for two months on the trail.

Maggie stared with the others. What she saw made her heart quake and her knees weaken. Her eyes darted right past the stockaded fortress. There—in the triangle between the rivers—the plain beneath the bluffs was crawling with Indians! Hundreds of tepees were spread out, their owners engaged in ritual dances.

She slumped against a stilled oxen, trying to gain strength from its solid, heaving side. How could she go near the fort? She was absolutely certain she could never face another Indian. It was an Indian who had abducted her, another Indian who had come too close to stealing her husband's affections from her forever. Her worst fears before her, the wagons screeched into movement again, and Maggie's body was forced to action. She had to follow the train.

The wagons were never actually driven right up to the fort. Instead, Chandler sent several men ahead on horseback to check on the grazing. They reported back that the Indians' animals had eaten all the grass surrounding Laramie. Chandler's train had to settle for a spot a good mile distant.

The storm had blown over, but it had also brought on the night, and it was dark when they settled in to cooking their meals. But from across the plains, the emigrants

35

heard more than the usual plaintive cries of a wolf pack. Tonight they were beset with the racket of hordes of Indians yelling, chanting, dancing.

Johnny had disappeared after he'd settled the oxen. He returned as Maggie was finishing the cooking. She stared at him, afraid to ask the question.

He answered it for her. "Sioux. We're far from Pawnee territory now, so you can ease up, Meg. They're dancing up a storm, all tricked out for war. Trying to get up enthusiasm to fight their local enemy, the Crow. They might fight the Snake, too. They were badly trounced by a Snake party last year."

Maggie shivered as the word *Snake* passed Johnny's lips.

He was watching her. "It will be cold tonight." He glanced around for his son. "Jamie! Run and get your mother's shawl. That's a good boy."

Maggie waited for Jamie's departure. "You know it's not the cold, Johnny. If it were, your strong arms would be more welcome protection than my shawl."

He ignored her hint, reaching for a piece of the jerky she was throwing into the stewpot. He bit into it. "I guess I do."

She shivered again, more at his indifference than from fear of Indians. She'd sooner take on twenty tribes of braves, single-handed, than Johnny's indifference. What was happening to him, to them? She would not beg for what should be given freely.

"What did they look like?"

"Different from the Indians in Red Eagle's village. These tribes came with their traveling houses. You saw the tepees. The women were fired up, too. Their faces were painted, and they had on their fancy dresses, beaded like yours. I think they'd all been drinking some pretty strong whiskey."

He paused to bring the picture back to his mind, choosing to ignore the obvious turmoil in his wife's face. He wasn't ready yet to unfetter his own emotions. He didn't understand them, anyhow. He hadn't understood much since Red Eagle and Snake.

"I met a man watching the Sioux—a white man. Said his name was Parkman. He was drunk, too, but I think it was with the sight, not the liquor. He kept saying it was a sight he'd come clear from New England to see. He called it a *rendezvous* and said more Sioux are due from all over the plains the next few days. He was aiming to stick around and follow them and watch the big battle. It all seemed a game to him. A funny kind of fellow— skinny, and with an unhealthy look, maybe even the lung fever. It's strange to come this far with no more purpose than to gawk at the Indians like they were savage freaks. It crossed my mind to give him a few words from experience, but he didn't seem the type to pay me any heed."

Before Maggie could respond, Jamie returned to place a shawl around his mother's shoulders.

"Thank you, son." She gave him a brilliant smile, a smile she'd been saving for Johnny. "Did you get something for yourself?"

"I couldn't find my old coat, Ma. This would be a good night for my new vest, though."

Maggie stirred the pot. "You know it's not finished yet."

She'd been putting it off, connecting even that vest in her mind with Red Eagle's village, and her dreams of an emaciated Jamie turned into a wild Indian waif. It had been more than two weeks since that incident. It was too soon to have the nightmare cleared from her mind. She looked up at her lingering husband. Would the nightmare ever free the two of them?

TOM tom tom tom, TOM tom tom tom.

The drumbeats echoed through her head, achingly, unceasingly. Maggie yelled out louder than necessary, trying to dull the sound. "Supper's on!" She tried to smooth the goosebumps from her arms. It didn't work.

In the cool of the morning, she began struggling with her hair. The steady winds kept pulling it from her grasp as she wove it into a long plait down her back, then rolled up the plait, pinning its heaviness to her head. It was an unexpected load, and she twisted her neck, trying to accustom herself to it.

She'd borrowed Gwen's piece of mirror for the task. She'd borrowed a big scarf from Grandma Richman, too. Now she took the scarf and carefully bound it round her head, turban-fashion.

Johnny came upon her at that moment. "What are you doing to yourself, woman?"

His face gleamed from the soap and water and razor he'd just used. Like the other men and women of the train, Johnny, too, was making preparations for the civilization beyond.

"Isn't it obvious? I'm covering my hair."

"Why?"

"You should be the last person to need to ask that question, Johnny Stuart."

Light dawned in his eyes. He came closer to put his arms around her in a rare gesture of solidarity. "You're afraid of its color. Afraid that what happened once may happen again."

"Yes!" every fiber of her being cried out.

Johnny kept one arm around her, but with his right hand began to slowly undo what she had so laboriously accomplished. "We've all got secret fears, Meg, myself included. But we can't escape from them by hiding. We've got to face them head on. We've got to try to overcome them. I'm going with you to Laramie. The Indians have other things on their minds than kidnapping a lovely white women with fire in her hair. Besides, they've brought their own squaws." He stopped. "You'll come as God made you, and I'll proudly show you off that way."

The turban was off, and her rich tresses flowed freely again. Maggie looked into the mirror and saw Johnny's face, his eyes reaching for hers. They met, and the stiffness went out of her body. He was willing to help her. She could do it. She turned and reached for his lips. They were warmer than they had been in days.

five

Fort Laramie was not what anyone had anticipated.

The Stuart family approached it on their two dray horses—Jamie, seated before his father, and Charlotte, trussed up on her mother's back, cross and fussing for her freedom. She was getting too big to be treated as a papoose. Lumbering behind on ropes were the oxen needing attention. In the radiance of the early summer morning the fort loomed before them, sparkling white beneath the sun, seemingly a worthy edifice for their hopes.

The Indian encampment was still spread out around it, all the way down to the water twenty-five feet below the rise on which the fort was built. In the light of day, the Sioux did not seem anywhere near as threatening as they had sounded in the night. Jamie was excited by those Indians who were up and about, mostly the indefatigable children and their mothers, looking the worse for the night's festivities. The braves were still in their tepees, sleeping off the party.

Maggie felt better and turned her attention back to Laramie itself. Fort John. No one called the quadrangle with fifteen-foot walls by its given name. But by any name it was imposing, rising as it did from the middle of nowhere. Its bastions stood tall at each corner, and sentried palisades hugged its walls.

Sooner than expected, the Stuarts were at the block-house and entering the gateway. They dismounted, looking around with eyes widened from days of empty prairies.

The interior did not correspond with the whitewashed brilliance of the fort's outside walls. All was a dry adobe brown, long since bleached of other colors by the relentless sun. Small buildings—houses—were built close against the walls, their doors and windows opening into a large central square. A corral to hold the animals in times of danger further partitioned off the space. There was a smithy and a shop selling stores. Lounging everywhere was as strange a collection of humanity as they'd yet set eyes upon.

Maggie watched her son's face as he took it all in—a dozen varieties of Indians, half-breeds, Mexicans, mountain men, even Creoles and Negroes surrounded them. There were men of every hue and dress, their attire adding strokes of color to the drab sandiness around them, the dialects and patois of their tongues imparting life to the heated stillness.

Johnny pressed them on so their gawking would insult no one. He was closing in on the blacksmith's shop. He had no desire to be at the end of a long line of emigrants wishing to use these services this day.

Nodding hello to the smith and his helpers, Johnny began negotiating for the shoeing of his animals and the purchase of bullets. His family continued to stare, even Maggie. The niceties of Independence became part of another lifetime.

"Ma," hissed Jamie. "Look at that one there. His buckskin is purple! And it's got bits of bright cloth stitched all over it!"

Maggie tried to appear worldlier than she was. "I guess he dyed it, son. The squares of cloth may be silk. It's shiny and soft enough. Looks a little like pictures of a clown I saw once in your father's books. He was called a Harlequin, and wore what they called motley, like that."

"Think he's a clown? Maybe he'll do some tricks if I ask."

"Hush. No, Jamie. He must be a hunter."

The boy's head was in a whirl. "See that Indian by the corral! I never saw one wearing such a colorful shirt."

Maggie took in the calico of the man in question. It had been trimmed with bright red fringes. There was a yellow sash around his waist and a matching turban with a feather sticking out from his hair.

"He must belong to a different tribe than we've yet met, Jamie. Just look, but don't say anything. We shouldn't appear too forward." She took the boy's hand and firmly moved him on to the store beyond. "Let's see if we can find some things we need. I lost my last big needle, and I have to ask about how to send a letter back to Ohio, to your grandparents."

"Is that what you were doing in the cabin last night, scribbling away?"

"I thought you were asleep."

"I was, mostly."

Jamie's attention was now switched to a group of mangy dogs lying in the center of the dusty street. "See. They have got dogs. I could've brought Bacon, after all!"

"No. Bacon's better off back at camp. He would've just gotten himself into mischief."

"I can't see how he's better off tied up like we left him. He hates being tied up."

"Someone had to guard the wagons, Jamie. That's his job."

They entered the dim interior of the company store at last. Maggie studied the rows of trade blankets, stacked according to value, the bins of flour and sugar and coffee.

She went up to a man behind the counter. "Excuse me, sir."

The clerk looked up from his ledger. It had been a long time between shaves and a bath, and his hair hung in greasy strings down his back.

"Could you give me the price for coffee, please?"

"Dollar a pint."

Maggie blanched. "How could that be?"

"This ain't Philadelphia, lady. Gotta haul in the goods from Santa Fe by mule train. Santa Fe brings 'em from farther down in Mexico, or even from Independence. Sugar's a dollar-fifty a pint, flour four bits a pint. Take it or leave it. Won't find no other goods a-settin' out on the trail up ahead, though." He went back to his ledger.

Maggie gathered her courage and spoke again. "What about vegetables, then? How much for potatoes? Or greens?"

The fellow gave her a curt laugh. "Ain't no veg-e-tables growed in Laramie. What you see is what we got. Staples, some cloth, blankets, ropes, Indian tradin' trinkets." He ran through the rest of the inventory in his head, then added, "Got some bacon slabs in the back room, too. Two dollars the pound. What'll it be?"

"Nothing just yet, thank you." Maggie gathered her son to her and made a hasty retreat to the street.

The clerk called after her. "How about some whiskey, lady? Seein' as how you're the first train of the season, I could let you have it for last year's prices, four dollars the pint!" His chortle of amusement was grating.

Blinded by the bright light, Maggie bumped into someone on the way out, but managed to beg the pardon of an
exotically beautiful woman. A woman, here? Spanish?

The woman shook her black tresses, murmured, "*De
nada*," and was gone.

Confused, Maggie returned to the smithy. Johnny was
closely watching a Negro farrier giving Dickens a new
pair of shoes.

She pulled her husband aside. "How much have we got
to spend, Johnny? Everything's terribly dear!"

Johnny wrinkled his brow. "After we see to the animals
and the ammunition, I've got to look into a new shaft for
the white-top. Sam thinks ours might not hold up over the
mountains ahead. I know the flour is running low, and
sugar, too, but it seems like coffee might be critical. It's
starting to taste more like chicory every day. Then we've
got costs up ahead to consider. Like guides and ferrying
for the Columbia River—"

"How bad is it, Johnny?"

He felt in his pockets and pulled out some carefully
hoarded gold coins. "Two twenty-dollar pieces is all I can
let you have, Meg. And it'll be tight at that."

She took the coins. "I'll do the best I can."

"You always do."

Back in the store, Maggie carefully marshaled her
resources and ordered, watching with eagle eyes to be
certain that her measures were fair. She was left with a
pitifully small pile of sacks and two copper pennies in her
hand.

Jamie was still hovering hopefully around a shelf filled
with trinkets which also encompassed a jar of sassafras
candy sticks. Maggie studied the wistful expression on

her son's face. She gave the clerk her last two coins—one for a needle, the other for five sticks of the candy.

Four of the sticks were carefully tucked away for emergencies down the road, but Jamie swaggered out with one in his mouth, like a cigar. Maggie had to smile as she watched the boy ape the men around him, hands tucked nonchalantly in his pockets, king of the mountain. Her heart went out to him for the world he must learn to grow into.

The Stuarts' errands were completed by afternoon, their horses loaded. But still they lingered, beginning to enjoy the crowded square. Neighbors from the train were everywhere. They waited in lines to have their horses or wagons tended, or just chatted with anyone who might have information about the trail ahead, or the states left behind.

It was here the Stuarts learned that their country was at war with Mexico. It was interesting information, but somehow distant from themselves. There was no news about the disposition of the Oregon Territory. That would have been more to the point, something they could understand. But even that information had become almost irrelevant. They were already on their way, and nothing would change that fact. The insularity of their trip was becoming overwhelming. Little mattered now but the trail itself, and its completion. What would come next was in a different universe.

Maggie and Johnny finally left through the gate's archway in late afternoon, satisfied to return to the known security of their own camp. Jamie unleashed a delirious Bacon and set off with Charlotte toddling beside him.

Johnny went about storing the new supplies and Maggie started a fire for supper.

It wasn't long before all of their dashed expectations began coming home to roost.

"No preacher. No priest. Nothing." Gwen threw down the frock she had slung over her arm, close to tears. "Just a bunch of dirty men spouting French and Mexican and Indian!"

Maggie picked up the wedding dress, admiring it as she dusted it off, folded it, and returned it gently to Gwen's arms. "It's lovely, Gwen. But hadn't you better put it in a safe place until it may be used?"

"When will that be?"

"There's always the Reverend Winslow."

"How can you even refer to that man as *reverend*? It would make me feel unclean to be wed by him!"

Maggie studied the water in her pot slowly coming to a boil. She threw in handfuls of jerky. "If your mind's made up on that account, then you'll have to wait. There's the Whitman Mission ahead. It's only another month or two. Johnny and I courted for seven years."

"But you were just children! I've already wasted half my life waiting!"

Maggie reached for her new bag of flour and grimaced at the unexpected activity within it. "Have you a sieve, Gwen? It's a pity to throw out anything of potential nourishment, but I for one can't stomach weevils in my dumplings."

Gwen turned, still pouting, to fetch one from her wagon.

Maggie called after her. "Besides, waiting will give you more time to be comfortable with each other, Gwen. It's only been sixty days since you met!"

"Never! It's been years out of my life!"

Maggie smiled into her pot, then frowned once more at her fifty-cent-a-pint flour. Nothing came easily or cheaply in this life.

Grandma Richman wandered up next, trailed by a passel of youngsters. She waved them off like so many flies. "Shoo, now! Jamie's over yonder with the Kreller girls. Go torture them for a while." She sank down next to Maggie, peering into the pot and flour bag. "See you sprung for some of Laramie's finest. Too bad you ain't got an egg or two to mix up with that. It'd make some mighty fine stew dumplings."

"I'm going to make some anyhow. My Jamie found a bird's nest yesterday. There were half a dozen eggs almost big as pullets. I'm just afraid what I'll find when I crack them open."

"Couldn't be worse than them weevils. You'd better eat that flour fast afore the bugs consume it all."

"My thoughts precisely."

Maggie leaned against the wagon and gave Grandma a closer inspection. She was beginning to look her age. The steel-gray bun had gone white. And lines had been added to the woman's face like so many miles traveled.

"I see Jube's got the splint off his arm. It took me by surprise. We haven't been talking much lately."

"I guess we been kind of caught up betwixt my troubles and yours. You come through them Injuns mighty fine. Better than I did at the fort today."

Maggie brushed hair from her eyes. "What happened?"

"I headed straight for that boor-gee-wa feller, the Frenchman in charge."

"Mr. Bourdeaux?"

"Guess so. I poked my head right into his quarters, and seed he didn't have naught for furnishin's, save a few doubtful women. Just a bunch of bearskins on the floor and a big old wardrobe. I told him he needed some first-class furniture so's he could live like the bigshot he was, and impress the lights outta them Spanish ladies." She sighed.

"He wasn't buying? Even for the *ladies*?" Maggie's mind flew back to the entrancing creature she'd met so briefly. What kind of life could there be at Laramie for a woman like that?

"We bartered, right enough. But I ended up with enough cloth to cover the seats of only half my younguns, a little flour, and a slab of bacon. That'll take us maybe into next week. He's gonna send his men for my grandma's dresser afore we leave at dawn tomorrow." Grandma snuffled, rubbed her nose on one voluminous sleeve, and trudged off.

Johnny's curiosity brought him over from his white-top. "What's going on here? That's the second female that's come by close to tears." He glanced around. "Oh, oh. Here's a third. I think I'll go borrow one of Irish's cheroots. It might chase away more than mosquitoes."

Hazel was closing in. "I told Max, Maggie."

Maggie handed her friend a mostly clean handkerchief and waved her into a sitting position. "Told him what?"

"You know, about—" Hazel snuffled into the cloth. "I've been so full of it, guess I thought everybody knew. Oh, Maggie, I'm going to have another bay-bee!" Pent-up tears finally flowed.

Gwen approached and took one look at Hazel. She shoved the sieve into Maggie's hand and beat a quick retreat.

With distaste written all over her face, Maggie attacked the flour, internally chiding herself. Why couldn't she handle a little thing like weevils? Here were these other women with real problems, and she was acting like some city girl who'd never seen a bug before. She dug a cup into the bag, but stopped stock still, her hand halfway to the sieve.

TOM tom tom tom, TOM tom tom tom.

The Indians had officially begun another night of revelry. Evidently they had to gear themselves up for facing troubles just the same as white folks. It made her feel some better, and brought the Indians within the realms of humanity.

"Another baby is not the end of the world, Hazel. Maybe you'll give Max a son this time. He'd probably like that."

"He'd love it. But I don't feel right about this one. I mean, my body doesn't, somehow. The girls felt right when I began to carry them, and straight on through to their birthing."

"It could just be all the rocks and dryness we've been traveling through, Hazel. More bounteous surroundings give a person a fuller feeling."

"And there weren't any trees at the fort, Maggie! Nothing green!" She was bawling again. "I'd been so longing for a touch of home!"

Maggie reached out a hand to touch Hazel's. Homesickness was running rampant through the train. Laramie was supposed to have cured that. It was supposed to have given them all strength for the next bad piece of trail. It had only made things worse.

"Would you like to eat with us tonight? The pot's big

enough. I'll just throw more in. And after, we'll get
Johnny to start some music. We really ought to give those
Indians a little competition."

Hazel dabbed at her eyes gratefully. "I haven't even
started our fire yet. I just couldn't face up to it. Being with
you all might take my mind off things."

"It might make the new baby happy, too. Like he's got
something joyous to grow toward."

Hazel blew her nose. "Bless you. Let me just go and
gather up my family."

Johnny finally judged it safe to come out of hiding.
"What've you got me into, Meg? I thought maybe we
might get some private time tonight to talk."

Maggie sighed. "I love you, Johnny, even though we
haven't been seeing eye to eye lately. There's nothing I'd
rather do than talk things out properly. But in this world
you can't always do what you want most. Gwen and Sam
are searching for bliss. Hazel's already had too much of
it. Grandma Richman's just looking to survive."

Her eyes moved across the circle. "And there's Ruth
Winslow, acting like she's lost her last friend in the world
and is ready to throw her Bible into the supper fire.
Laramie obviously didn't come up to her expectations,
either. And where was the Reverend today? I didn't see
him at the fort at all. It was Ruth standing in line at the
smithy for repairs. Can't that man ever give her any
support? At the least, I expected to see him standing on a
box in the middle of the square, preaching to the fallen
women."

Johnny lowered himself next to her, grinding out the last
bit of his unaccustomed cigar. "Can't you forget about your
orphans for just a little while? What about us?"

Maggie sank back from the pot onto her haunches. "I'll be satisfied to keep you with me for another hundred years, body and soul."

He reached for her lips, touching them gently, sweetly. "That's asking far more than anyone else."

"I'll compromise and try to be content right now if you would only take on the chore of cracking Jamie's eggs into this bowl. I can't face any more broken dreams today."

six

The whole train was held up the next morning, waiting for men from the fort to come and unload Grandma Richman's cherry chest. They arrived at last, but took their good time completing the job, cussing and complaining as if they were unused to manual labor.

When the fort's buckboard was on its way back to the gates of Laramie and the apartments of the bourgeois, the fort's leader, and when Grandma's wagon was reloaded, the Chandler Party finally pulled out. As the last of the train wended its way from the shining walls of civilization, none could resist looking back a final time.

Maggie gaped at what she saw. It wasn't the occasional group of Sioux who were still straggling in to their rendezvous that so surprised her. It was what came from beyond.

Beyond was another wagon train of emigrants. And it was a big one—twice the size of theirs—and still growing, like a serpent with an endless tail in the haze across the plain.

Chandler's train worked harder than ever that day. It stopped a shorter time for the noon break and made camp later in the afternoon. No one admitted they were in competition with the new party, but it was so. They were in competition for the dry grass and sparse water ahead.

On the second day out from Laramie, in mid-afternoon, they met up with a few lone travelers coming from the west. The forms took shape slowly on the horizon. At first the small group was taken for Indians, perhaps scouts from one of the tribes at enmity with the Sioux. Where there were Indian scouts, there could be unfriendly hunting or war parties close behind.

The men pulled out their rifles and walked with them, but the wagons kept moving. Eventually they could see that the group ahead was not Indian at all, for it was followed by pack animals.

The Reverend Josiah Winslow strained his eyes harder than the others to make out the details. Could this be his fate coming to meet him? Danite scouts from Brigham Young? He fingered his silver pistols expectantly as the two groups finally came together, east meeting west.

The train stopped. Everyone gathered around the newcomers, anxious to learn what they could of the land ahead, firsthand. Maggie stared at the grizzled old-timer in charge. Winslow stared, too, then breathed once more and dropped his fingers from the guns. He was saved, yet again.

The old-timer must have been in the wilderness forever, Maggie figured. His buckskins were shiny with grease, the leggings japanned a fine black enamel from constant daily use. Word filtered through the crowd of men that this was the legendary Jim Bridger himself!

Maggie pushed with her children to get a better view and stared with awe at the man whose exploits had gained him notoriety even back home. Finally she began to pick up bits of the conversation.

His voice was thick with disuse, but rich and strong. "Mighty pleasant to hear the busy hum of our own language again. Ain't had much use for it these past weeks. Come over from California, the hard way."

Johnny was questioning him. "Did you hear anything of the conflict between the States and Mexico while you were in California?"

Bridger shrugged and grinned. "Don't pay much mind to foolish politickin'. Last I heard, Fremont was settin' up to make a big man of hisself out there. Took over some unprotected towns in the name of the U.S. of A. Can't think what the Mexicans thought. It's mighty easy country out there in Californy, and mostly the local Spanish folks just let things slide."

He'd dismounted from his horse and was giving it its head near some scruffy buffalo grass. "Wouldn't happen to have any coffee about, would you? It's been a coon's age since I tasted a cup."

Maggie could see Chandler thinking hard. It was not nearly time to call a halt for the day, but they did have in hand someone who could give them critical information about the land ahead, tips that might make the difference between life and death. Finally decided, he motioned for camp to be set up.

Maggie was the first to get a fire going and start up a fresh pot of coffee. She knew Johnny wanted a better chance to talk to this man. She'd barely presented Bridger and his party with a boiling pot of the drink when chaos started in again. Bridger had been talking about buffalo.

"Sure I seed some. Nice herd, not five miles ahead. Was moving fast away from the trail, though. Seen it happen afore. They've already smelt you coming." He sipped the scalding brew and touched his finger to his slouch hat in Maggie's direction. "Plumb refreshin', ma'am."

Sam plunged in. "We be a little short on meat. Any chance of us catching up with them?"

"Iffen you got some good, fresh horses. But you got to outsmart 'em now they knows you be here. They ain't the brightest of creatures, but got self-preservation instincts nevertheless."

"How would you go about doing that . . . outsmarting the buffalo, I mean?" Johnny asked.

"Use a huntin' maneuver called 'ringing.' Good for wild horses, too. Gotta circle 'em, all around, from a far enough distance so's they don't suspect, then move in slow and keep headin' off their escape paths till they get tired out. Won't be headin' too much farther west, this partic'lar herd, 'cause the Injuns done started in settin' prairie fires from that end to confine 'em. I just passed through a couple days of smoke haze on that account. Be headin' south, the buffalo are." He noticed the fire of interest in Johnny's eyes. "Ever caught you any?"

"Three."

"Ain't bad for a easterner. Might be talked into a little hump meat myself."

"You'd go with us, sir?" Johnny's question was rife with excitement.

"Ain't nobody ever called me 'sir.' Name's Jim, son. And my half-breed pony is clean fed up with trekkin'. Him and me both could stand a little excitement."

That cinched it. Maggie watched her husband and the other men race to prepare their best horses. They were little boys again, off to hunt with the master. She fervently prayed Bridger would bring them luck. It took a lot of meat to keep a hundred people going strong. More to the point, she prayed that Johnny would control his new inner excitement and return unharmed.

The hours passed slowly for the women and children left behind. There were endless chores to catch up with, but Maggie found herself turning her glance again and yet again toward the southwest where the hunters had disappeared.

It was not until long after nightfall that they heard the sounds of returning horses. Maggie had given up and was dozing in the caravan with her children. She quickly pulled a shawl around her shoulders and went out to replenish her fire.

The men straggled in slowly on exhausted mounts. But on the rump of each horse, and on pallets dragged behind, were slabs of buffalo meat. Maggie watched with growing excitement until Johnny finally appeared near the end of the group, riding on one side of Bridger. His horse was laden, too.

She rushed up. "What happened?"

His grin was big enough to light up the night. "I learned a few things about hunting this day. How to look for buffalo traces, and elk beds, and a fair amount about butchering and packing, too."

He slid off his weary horse and began to relieve it of its heavy load. "Jim taught us how to make carrying sacks from the skins right there at the kill, and he's going to cook up a special recipe for us tonight!"

Maggie's gaze passed to the older man who was obviously enjoying his role as mentor.

"Got you a bright young man there, missus. Ready to learn an' easy to teach. Give me a season or two, could make a decent mountain man outten him."

Maggie's response was quick. "Consider yourself welcome to stop by and continue the lessons anytime you're in Oregon, Mr. Bridger."

He chuckled. "Smart lady to get your hooks in first. Just like a few mama grizzlies I been up against." He dismounted. "Time to start in crackin' them buffalo bones. Had me a little treat of warm buffalo brains out by the kill, but it hardly whetted my appetite. Got a yen for some 'trapper's butter,' an' I'll make you some soup like you never yet et. Got your fires up, Missus?"

Maggie couldn't help smiling as she led Bridger to her camp. The years of wilderness had not blunted the old man's innate sense of humor. And Johnny's reputation would be soaring again now that Bridger had chosen their fire at which to sup. She took a minute to wake Jamie from his sleep. The boy should not miss the doings. It would be a story he could tell his own children—the night he ate supper with Jim Bridger.

Maggie watched carefully as the trapper flagellated buffalo bones with his hatchet, then scooped out the marrow within. He kept a bit aside for his 'butter,' but tossed the rest, over a pound, into a gallon of water he'd instructed her to heat almost to boiling over the fire.

While the hump—the most tender part of the buffalo—was being broiled next to it, Bridger carefully added to the pot blood he'd saved from the cavity of the animal. Finally he tossed in quantities of salt and black pepper. Soon it was the consistency of a rice soup and pronounced ready to eat. Tin cups were passed around and everyone tasted of the strangely rich concoction.

Bridger sighed as he slurped. "Best to throw some ribs up

against the fire, and sling a hunk of brisket into that cauldron when the soup's gone. I'll assure you we'll eat till the day peeps forth. We be carnivorous animals. The marrow and fatness and lifeblood of this wholesome beast be good for us." He grinned. "Ain't nothin' like the buffalo to make your face shine with grease and gladness."

Maggie started with wonder at his words, but obliged him. Soon the soup was gone and they'd moved on to the hump. The diners were, indeed, greasy and full and happy. Jamie had stared in silent awe, eaten his fill, and promptly fallen asleep. Johnny took the boy back to his bed, returning to his seat between Maggie and Sam, ready to fasten his attention back on Bridger.

The old trapper harkened back to California again. "Now, be you good and wary up ahead near the South Pass. Won't be no Injuns lyin' in wait, but be some humans of more devious ways. I met up with 'em and their group comin' up past the Sierras. Straight by the Humbolt River they come, salt desert an' all. It be some of the meanest, ghastliest, godforsakenest country ye ever seed or imagined."

Bridger slowly caught all their faces around the fire, making sure he had their full attention. "Name of Hastings and Hudspeth, these types, and they're set on talkin' decent folks like you offen the Oregon Trail onto their own cutoff down to California. They're all het up to get more Americans into their country so's they can slice it off from Mexico."

"They'd be hard put to talk us out of our objective at this point," commented Johnny.

Bridger gave him a level look. "Ain't as easy as all that, son. You come a fair piece so far, but it don't hold a candle to the mean country up ahead. Time you get to South Pass, you'll be thinkin', 'Anythin's better than more o' this.' That's when Hastings and company pop up, like, an' start a-whisperin' in your ear 'bout their own brand o' promised land. Talkin' 'bout how it'll take a month off the journey, and the country at the end full of milk an' honey."

He licked a finger, and continued with great seriousness. "There'll be some among you who'll be tempted. Might even be some defections. Sure as shootin', be lots of talk and fightin' over it. But mind my words. *There ain't no easier way.* The Oregon way be rough, but Hastings's cutoff be death."

Bridger's information was digested as the old man leaned toward the fire. "Those ribs look just about done to me. Like 'em when they're still good an' juicy. Carve up a hunk an' pass it over."

It was a strange night. The wolves surrounded them, howling more aggressively than ever, longing for scraps from the great kill that they smelled. The evening star had disappeared and the morning star was blinking on the horizon. The very air was filled with comradeship and prophecy. They would, indeed, eat until the dawn.

Bridger finally rolled himself up in his skins and slept for a few short hours before taking his leave for Laramie. He left behind a groggy camp, trying to deal with not enough sleep and the need to preserve the bounty that remained from their hunt.

It was not until afternoon that the remaining meat was jerked, the green skins cleaned, and the train rolled on its way again toward South Pass. Time was growing short. It was late June. The winter snows would not be long in coming.

In the days ahead, it became harder and harder to conceive of winter snows. The desert land with its heat and aridity seared everyone and everything. Wagons began to groan more loudly as wood dried out, leaving cracks for more dust to enter, putting greater strain upon critical joints. White-tops began to break down. Oxen thinned and struggled for each new step. Ravens, buzzards, wolves—all manner of creatures of carrion—haunted their days . . . and their dreams at night.

seven

The Stuarts' wagons had rotated to the front of the line at last. Now they were enjoying a brief respite from the dust of the trail behind. It was Jamie—one of the few still enjoying the daily experience—who spotted a new kind of prairie civilization. He'd been foraging ahead with Bacon and came running back, just before noon, in high excitement.

"There's acres and acres of them!"

Johnny mopped his brow. "Acres of what, Jamie?"

"The funniest little animals. Like squirrels without bushy tails. And they talk to each other! They've got a whole city up ahead. But Bacon barked and they all disappeared down little holes, and—"

"Whoa! Could be prairie dogs. Go ask Mr. Chandler if it's time to halt. It might be fun for everyone to see."

Jamie raced off, and soon they'd stopped, a short walk from the prairie dog village. Maggie cobbled together a quick meal and the whole family set out to investigate Jamie's find.

They met the Krellers coming back, stepping carefully through the abrasive scrub brush.

"See anything, Max?"

He shook his head no. "They were scared off by too many folks butting in, Johnny. Only thing we spied was a good-sized rattler heading for one of the holes, a little 'dog' half shoved down his mouth. It upset the girls."

Johnny was interested. "Didn't you try to catch it,

Max? Bridger said rattlers make good eating."

Max paused to knock the dottle from his pipe. "I can stomach a lot of things these days, but rattlesnake ain't one of them."

Hazel, coming up behind her husband, was obviously relieved by his words. "And thank heaven for that, too. My insides are queasy enough these days." She grabbed for her daughter. "Don't lallygag behind like that, Miss Matty! Not with snakes running loose."

Maggie studied Hazel. "Try and take a little rest out of the sun until we leave."

Hazel smiled wanly at her friend's concern. "I fully intend to. But the girls wouldn't let me be till I'd seen this new wonder. It turned out just like the rest of the elephant."

Jamie pulled at Maggie's arm. "Come on, Ma. We'll creep up silent as Injuns, then get on our stomachs. They'll come out if we're real quiet."

That's what they did. Charlotte had fallen asleep in the heat, under the shade of a piece of cloth Maggie had rigged up on her carrier. It was very peaceful lying there with Johnny on one side and Jamie, silent for once, on the other.

Before them spread a vast area of hard-packed dirt, pocked with little creature-made holes and hills. The only sound came from flies droning lazily above. Maggie tried to imagine what it looked like beneath, in the dark tunnels and rooms. She pictured a vast underground city, everyone busy doing his job.

Funny how creatures had jobs to do the same as humans. And these particular creatures needn't ever pack their bags, load their wagons, and move farther on. From the looks of things, they'd been here for centuries and planned to continue for a few more. How nice to be settled down for good and final this way. She closed her eyes and sighed.

Jamie nudged her. Maggie opened her eyes to follow his pointing finger. Not fifteen yards away, a little brown sentry had poked his head above one of the holes. Maggie watched with interest as he swiveled his head nervously this way and that, tiny pointed ears twitching. He finally scurried out to stand on hind legs at the edge of his burrow, black tail a tremble, alert. Satisfied that the giant marauders had gone, the creature let out a shrill whistle, and a half dozen others popped out of holes around him. Soon there were scores of prairie dogs carrying on their daily routine in front of the Stuarts—chatting, scolding, playing. It was fascinating, almost as good as watching the actors in the theater where Johnny had once taken Maggie in Cincinnati.

But within an instant, they were all gone, scattered back into their underground sanctuaries. There'd been no noise or motion from the four Stuarts. What had frightened the creatures? Maggie silently sought Johnny's eyes, riveted on a hole perhaps six feet from them.

Very slowly a rattlesnake inched his way out. It was engorged. It should not have been moving at all, should have been curled up somewhere for a week to digest its vast meal. Perhaps it was seeking the sun for this process.

Maggie suddenly realized that Johnny's fingers were reaching for the hunting knife stuck in his belt. Her throat was too dry to cry out for him to stop. In a moment he had the weapon in his grasp. In another, he'd leaped up and pinioned the rattler with the sharp blade through the top of its head. Maggie swallowed, hard.

Jamie let out a whistle. "Nice going, Pa! Guess we get fresh meat for supper!"

Johnny grinned as he slowly pulled the rest of the body from its hole. He held it up before him, measuring its length with his eyes. "A good two yards. Must be a granddaddy. His skin will make a nice belt for you, son, and maybe enough left over to tie around that hair of yours. It's growing so fast you're starting to look like a young Sioux."

The thought of getting his hands on his very own rattlesnake skin was too much for Jamie. "Yahoo! Guess we can head on back now, right, Pa? I figure you've done the prairie dogs a big favor, but I also figure they won't be coming out for a while to thank you."

Johnny mussed his son's sun-bleached hair. "You probably figure right. It's time to move on." He looked toward Maggie for her assessment of his prowess.

She gulped. "*You* are skinning and cooking that thing tonight, Johnny Stuart!"

"I expected as much. It's lucky you weren't along on the buffalo hunts, Meg, although a good squaw always trails along with her man to clean up after."

"That's just one of the reasons I chose to come back with you from a certain Pawnee village."

He walked next to her, the dead rattler slung over a shoulder. "And here I was thinking it was my sheer strength of character coming through at last."

She had to smile. "It was a little of that, too."

"What are you talking about, Pa?"

Johnny had his free arm around his wife and still-sleeping daughter. "Never mind, son. You'll grow up soon enough."

Jamie scuffed pebbles before him, grumbling. "That's what you always say."

The rattlesnake stew was not half bad. But afterwards, with the children asleep, it seemed to keep Maggie wakeful, her head buzzing. "We haven't finished talking it all out yet, Johnny."

His drowsy head poked up from his blanket. "What?"

"You did it again today. You acted instinctively. Dangerously."

"You'd rather starve?"

"That, that *thing* was within a single body length of us. It could have struck out at you, at any of us."

"It had a full belly, and other matters on its mind."

"But what if, Johnny? What if?"

He sighed and rolled back to his side of the bedroll. "This trip has been teaching me that life is nothing more than a lot of ifs. Should we stop to consider each one, we'd never get anywhere, much less to Oregon. Things have happened to each of us, even between us, but we're still alive, Meg. Our children are thriving. You can't ask for anything more. And you can't ask me to stop and seriously consider every move I make in the future. I'm not just a bookman anymore!"

He was propped up on an elbow now. "Sometimes events take over. There's no time for working out the logic, like so many ancient Greeks sitting around the marketplace diagramming life and eternity. We're making a new world out here, Meg. There's no room for philosophers in it, only for the man of action."

Maggie sat up. The moon pricked through their tent

here and there, softly outlining her face.

"It's just that . . . well, you weren't the one left in that Pawnee village, Johnny. You weren't the one who had to think for hours—hours that seemed more like eternity—of the real possibility of spending the rest of your days in that place. Staying there with people who would only understand you so far, and never any farther. At moments like that, books and the life we had planned for ourselves in Oregon . . . they all seemed very important. You remember, Johnny! We talked it over so many times! We'd build a real house for ourselves at last. We'd set up the press and maybe begin a little newspaper. We'd bring words into a raw place. Words soften the rough edges of things. They make people more human . . . more as God intended us to be."

"I haven't changed the plan, Meg. I might do it with a little more aplomb, is all."

She looked down into his dark eyes, onto the outline of his face. "Are you sure?"

Anger spread over that face. An anger she was unused to seeing. "Can't you understand? I'm not sure of *anything* anymore!"

He hardly heard her return, it was so low, so halting. "Not even *God*? Not even . . . us?"

Johnny's anger faded. "You're trying me badly, but I think I'll keep you for another little while."

Maggie knew his last words had been in jest. She lay back in the dark, watching her husband sleep, satisfied for the moment.

eight

The Chandler Party laid over at Independence Rock for the Fourth of July. The massive outcrop of granite had risen ahead of them for days, giving them strength to move forward. The Platte was behind, the Sweet Water River by the Rock sorely needed. Before noon, camp was organized between the Rock's base and the river, freeing the livestock to roam toward the water.

The women immediately set in to their washing, Fourth of July or not. The men, however, commenced to celebrate. Jarboe, Smith, and Simpson had chipped in for a jug of white lightning at Laramie. Now they unplugged it and too generously offered it around. By mid-afternoon, most of the men and older boys were feeling uproarious. They were shooting at targets for wagers, setting up wrestling matches, and otherwise letting off steam. Even Johnny, who never touched the stuff, had succumbed.

He sauntered over to his white-top—already decorated with Charlotte's drying linens—in search of further ammunition. His step was jauntier than usual, and a silly grin was plastered on his face.

Maggie stared. Thanks to Bridger, Johnny was full of himself these days. And Chandler was still feeling the slight of not entertaining the great mountain man at his own fire. It was an understandable position. As elected leader of the group, Chandler would expect some benefits. But the hatchet ought to be buried before it grew into something larger.

Johnny rooted around in his open wagon, making Maggie wonder what he would be up to next. When her husband went after the little barrel of pine tar and hog fat used to grease the wagon axles, she figured she knew.

"Are you going to add your name to the Rock, Johnny?"

"Why not? Jamie's been pestering me. He wants to find a spot close to Fremont's own name. Why don't you bring the baby and come along with us?"

"Someone's got to do the work, Johnny."

He looked at her, his eyes glazed from his unusual imbibing, his fingers twitching with the need to find more and better excuses for adventure. "You've done enough. Ease up, woman. Charley'll have a clean bottom for another week. A little more dirt won't hurt the rest of us."

"What about the supper? The women were planning on a picnic meal—"

"You can make some porridge. We've no dearth of that these days." He dragged her away from the fire she'd just been laying out, and Charlotte toddled after.

When the child stumbled and fell, Maggie broke away from her husband and carried her daughter the remainder of the way to the wall of rock.

Jamie was already there, marveling at the inscriptions as high as his neck could crane to see, reading some off to a crowd of admiring youngsters. "This fellow Whelan must have been a sailor. He's left an anchor for his mark. And there's lots of ladies' names." He turned to his approaching father. "Did that many ladies come already, Pa?"

"That would be poetic exaggeration, son, or maybe just wishful thinking. I suspect men added their sweethearts' names, as a sort of reminder. Like I'm fixing to do now.

Although my mark'll be a little different because your mother is actually making the trip." He smiled. "A fact she'll not let me forget."

Johnny shoved the stick into the gunk and laboriously began to paint an inscription. Maggie watched as it grew:

JOHN STUART, 4 JULY, 1846
4—BUFFALO
MAGGIE STUART
1—PAWNEE CHIEF

"What kind of inscription is that?"

He grinned at his wife as she removed Charlotte's fingers from the grease.

"Score-keeping, you might say."

Maggie wasn't sure she wanted to be remembered to posterity by that particular inscription. Is that how Johnny now chose to recall the whole incident? But it was done.

"Me too, Pa! Don't forget me!"

Johnny handed the stick to Jamie. "Write it yourself, boy. You're big enough and able."

Jamie took the stick and added:

JAMIE AND BACON AND BABY C. WAS HERE TO.

"Leaves something to be desired, grammar-wise, but the point is made." Johnny turned to the boy. "You are now in charge of your sister. See that you keep her out of the hog grease. Your mother and I are going to climb this rock." And leaving the boy complaining, Johnny grabbed his rifle and his wife and took off in search of a reasonable access point.

Maggie protested all the way up, but once on top, lay flat on her stomach admiring the view. Ahead of them more bluffs of rock stuck up from the land, hazy in the sun.

"That would be the Devil's Gate just ahead, Meg. They say the Sweet Water barrels through the narrow canyon something fierce. We'll have to go around it."

He was easier now, the climb having burned off some of the alcohol in his blood. His eyes were almost back to normal. Maggie fervently hoped the jug was finished and no more would appear. She knew the men needed a little diversion, but this kind of behavior was unacceptable to her. She'd thought Johnny had felt the same . . . until this trip. Besides, Hal Richman's death was still in her mind. She tried to push that thought back, swiveling around on the smooth surface to look toward the East, from whence they'd come. There was a trail of dust rising from the hard-packed wagon grooves in the distance.

"More emigrants coming," Johnny noted for her. "They must have moved right on out from Laramie. They ought to join up with us tonight if they keep at it."

"Then we won't be the first anymore."

"Does it bother you?"

Maggie raised her shoulders and let them drop in a silent shrug. "I know it shouldn't, but it does."

"So you've finally invested some sentiment in our undertaking."

"What are you talking about, Johnny? I've invested everything in this journey!"

"That's not what I mean. You're getting caught up in it. In the idea itself. Being first for the season is all part of that."

"I had something more in mind . . . like being first for what little grass remains up ahead."

He slung an arm around her casually. "I'll have to try and break you of this worrying habit, Meg. There's no point in it whatsoever."

"Easy for you to say," she shot back, more crossly than she'd anticipated. "Have you taken a hard look at Checkers and Brandy recently? They are not thriving. Other folks have extra teams. We've been working all of ours right along. Lose the animals, and you'll be adding your precious printing press and type to the pile of discarded dreams along the trail."

Johnny withdrew his arm. "I expected a little more enthusiasm on the Fourth. Here we are striking out for new territory, expanding boundaries—"

"Since when have you taken a patriotic view of this whole enterprise? I thought we'd dropped most of that when the '54-40' signs began wearing off the other wagons!"

"Margaret McDonald Stuart." He sighed. "I can't seem to say anything right to you today. Maybe it's best just to give it all a rest for a while." He inched his way into an upright position. "Would you care to take my free arm on the way down, or have you enough righteous anger left to manage it on your own?"

"I'm not convinced you'll be seeing straight enough to be of much assistance."

"*Ouch.* Each word thrusts like an arrow. Pawnee. Straight to my heart." He started sliding down. "I will leave you, then, madam." And he did.

The day did not improve for Maggie. She returned to her children and her wagons with fresh bruises from the descent. From a distance, she watched—ungraciously—the new group of wagons pull into the Chandler camp while other members of their party milled around the newcomers, anxious to socialize on this most gregarious of days.

Long after she'd gotten the children to sleep, the sound of guns fired in random bursts of enthusiasm still peppered the night. It was beginning to seem like a waste of good ammunition.

Johnny had not returned to their camp, and Maggie had ignored the picnic, feeding the children their evening meal alone for the first time in months. Then she'd sat by the fire, stitching on Jamie's Indian vest.

It was Gwen who finally approached, looking like she had something to spill, but afraid to let it out. She sat down by Maggie, too casually. "I haven't seen you at any of the festivities."

"There were things that needed doing."

"Apparently." Gwen waited a few long moments. "You haven't met any of the newcomers yet, I gather?"

"No."

"Pleasant enough group of people, for the most part—"

Maggie pulled her eyes from her stitching. It was mostly a charade anyway. It was far too dark to continue with the sewing. "What's on your mind, Gwen?"

It poured out. "You really should be at the dancing, Maggie. The new people—the Donner Party?—they've got a fresh widow with them. Young. Pretty. And she's not mourning too hard."

"So?"

"Use your head, Maggie! Need I spell it out for you? She's making a play for every man in sight. Especially your Johnny. He's danced with her thrice already!"

Maggie pricked herself with the needle. "If she's that

dangerous, you'd best be heading back to Sam, hadn't you?"

Gwen flounced up. "I'm sure I don't know what's gotten into you lately! I will be getting back to Sam. But if it were my man out there dancing with that Annabelle thing, I surely wouldn't be sitting all alone here!"

Maggie waited till Gwen had disappeared toward the other end of the campground. The music she'd been trying to ignore came more clearly than ever to her ears. She lifted the pricked finger to her lips and sucked on it. She was being as stubborn as a mule, and she knew it.

Finally, she got up and peeked in at the safely sleeping children. Bacon was on watch and gave her a silent wag of his tail, as if to say, "Don't be silly. I'll take care of my charges. Go where you're needed.'

She went at last. But she did not immediately penetrate to the light of the fires around the musicians and dancers. She stood, instead, in the shadows of a wagon, picking out the new faces before her, searching for the woman who was after her husband.

It didn't take long for her eyes to find the two. They were dancing again. For the fourth time? Or was it the fifth? Where was Johnny's sense? Didn't he know that a man danced only once—and perfunctorily at that—with any woman but his own? There would be talk starting already.

She couldn't tear her eyes from their figures. The woman was, indeed, attractive. She was tiny, with darkly flowing hair that swirled around her petite, but evident, charms. Johnny seemed to be entranced. The new party must have brought more whiskey with them. There were jugs sitting around on the ground. Johnny had obviously helped himself. He was more animated than she could ever remember seeing him.

She and Johnny had never danced like that together. They'd never danced at all. It was not something in the frame of Maggie's experience. Her father had forbade such expressions, and their traveling ways had never brought them to such a social before. She wasn't even sure she could dance. Not like that woman out there.

Maggie continued to stare while newborn emotions sprang up in her breast. If she'd stop to figure them out, she'd know that chief among these emotions was jealousy. But she did not stop. Instead, she pulled at the pins remaining in her hair and shook it all out. Before she could change her mind, she emerged from the shadows and strode into the midst of the merrymakers. She was about to create a scene, and she felt just fine about it.

Her eyes flashed as she walked by Johnny and the widow. But she didn't interrupt them. She moved past, to where a handsome man was standing, cheroot in hand. He was dressed like a gambler, his cherry vest and string tie flashy in the glints of light, his whole person impeccable, as if he'd just stepped off a flourishing riverboat.

Dark eyes drank in Maggie's form with interest. The cheroot was dropped and he bowed low. "Would you favor me with a dance, mademoiselle?"

"It is *madam*, but it would be my pleasure, indeed."

And they were off, swinging into the revelry, Maggie's eyes catching the frowns of disbelief on the faces of Irish and Sue standing nearby. She had made a good choice. The man could dance. He led her feet carefully, smoothly in pursuit of his own. For a moment Maggie forgot her purpose and actually began to enjoy herself.

Then his hands enclosed her waist more tightly, his lips whispering close to her ear. "Who are you? You came from out of the night like some mysterious, beautiful wraith. I think you've enchanted me."

Before Maggie could answer, the music stopped. The firm hands began to lead her away but were interrupted.

"I'll thank you to unhand my wife, sir!"

The older man—he must have been almost forty, for Maggie could now see specks of gray decorating his sideburns—turned on Johnny. They were the same height, but the gambler's breadth was greater. He gave a smile of superiority. "Perhaps you'd best learn to tend your own henhouse before turning to others, young man."

Maggie saw Johnny's fingers ball up, and before she could stop him, his fist had shot out, squarely into her partner's patrician nose.

Unbelieving, Maggie waited for what would happen next. It took no time at all. A fine linen handkerchief was removed from a pocket to dab at the injured nose. It was returned with a small flourish, followed by a great fist that smashed into Johnny's face, sending him reeling to the ground.

Aghast, Maggie stared at the grinning stranger. His face had a wicked cast in the night light.

He offered a hand to her, and she could see that it was clean, uncalloused by any work on the trail. "The music begins again. Would you care to join me?"

Maggie shook her head dumbly and sank down next to her husband. She was out of her league. She'd been foolish to start this thing. Maggie tugged at Johnny but he didn't move. He'd been knocked unconscious.

Other hands came to her rescue. Soon Sam and Irish

were hoisting Johnny between them, and Max was gently taking her arm, leading her back to their own camp.

Johnny was propped by the fire, and Sam paused before her. "You don't want to be messing around with that man, Maggie. Goes by the name of Jack Gentry, but I suspicion he's had others. He ain't like us. Lots of them ain't like us." Sam turned his eyes on Johnny who was now snoring gently. "He'll be feeling his head in the mornin', but should come back to his right senses."

Maggie was left alone with her husband. She was still angry, not only with his choice of partners, but also with his attempts to stop her from the very thing he'd been doing himself. They'd never played at double standards before. It was upsetting and frightening.

She banked the fire, slung a buffalo robe over Johnny, and went to sleep in the wagon with the children.

nine

When the Chandler Party traveled past Devil's Gate the next day, Johnny was in no mood to enjoy it. They stopped for the nooning on the far side, and several members of the group went off to explore the chasm. Johnny just collapsed in a sorry heap next to the fire.

Maggie was not sympathetic. She had other things on her mind. The Donner Party had elected to travel in tandem with Chandler's group, and aside from *la belle* widow—who'd been snooping around their fire that morning, offering unwelcome solace to Maggie's husband—she'd picked up quite a bit of additional gossip on the new people.

As Sam had said, they were a different breed. That gambler's hands had been soft and clean because he'd hired someone to drive his wagon. Most of the members of the Donner Party appeared very well off, indeed. Each family traveled with two or three wagons and hired drovers. Their well-kept women were stuffed into couches from whence they sniffed at salts and perfumes to keep the dust of the road from touching their dainty nostrils. They probably had gold bars secreted under their wagon beds. They certainly had no dearth of food. One of the men was even rumored to have brought his entire cellar of fine French wines and brandies with him.

Maggie, miffed at such largess in a world of hunger and struggle, hoped it would all turn to vinegar. In short, her mood had not improved with the new day.

Johnny finally stirred, groaned, and raised his head. "I didn't know you could dance."

"I can't. Where did *you* learn?"

"I had to do something all those long winters in the cities with my pa."

"*Ha*! And you told me you spent them pining for me!"

"Well, I did some of that, too."

"Not enough, apparently."

"Come on, Meg. What's wrong with a little harmless dancing?"

"What you were doing with that woman last night was not harmless!"

"You were off in a wretched humor. What was I supposed to do?"

"Come and get me out of my wretched humor! Maybe even teach me how to dance." Maggie banged her spoon against the porridge pan. The stuff really was becoming disgusting.

Jamie strolled up with Charlotte in tow, took one peek into the pot, and grimaced. "Porridge again? People over to the Donners are eating bacon, and real bread, and *jam*."

"*We* are eating porridge again." She slammed some into a dish and shoved it at him. "Here."

Jamie looked at his mother, then his father. "Is the day after the Fourth always like this? 'Cause if it is, I think I'll pass on the Fourth next year."

Neither of his parents laughed, or even smiled. Jamie took his plate and rambled off in the direction of the Donner Party. Maybe someone would take pity on him and slap a little jam on top.

Johnny ignored the oatmeal and went off into the grass to seek a quiet brooding place. Maggie spooned porridge into Charlotte, put her into the wagon for a nap, and walked back out.

Her glance took in both their wagons and all their earthly possessions. Was it really worthwhile, this thing they were doing? Would the printing press Johnny had salvaged so long ago ever make it to Oregon? If it did, would they—she and Johnny—still be working together as a team, or would their current differences pull them yet further apart?

Maggie was fixing to allow herself a good cry when a movement caught her eye near the front of Johnny's wagon. Had he returned to fuss with the traces? He'd been complaining that one of them was developing a crack.

No. Even with their fight and his hangover, Johnny would not be moving so stealthily. Maggie strode over to see for herself what was going on. Fight or no, this was still Stuart territory, hers as well as Johnny's.

As she rounded the corner of the white-top, she caught sight of a head pulled swiftly from the front opening. The man straightened himself to his full height and faced her.

"Mr. Gentry! Have you any particular reason for poking into affairs obviously not your own?"

"Ah, the fair Mrs. Stuart! So you've discovered my name."

His voice was oily today. Maggie trusted him even less than the night before.

"And you mine," she shot back.

"It is a small world, after all, this mutual camp of ours." He brushed back his full head of hair, trying to disguise the grease he'd gotten upon his pristine fingers.

"Riding with our train gives you no right to trespass."

"I was merely . . . seeking your husband. To inquire after his health."

"It would have been far better without the intervention of your fist last night."

Gentry chose to appear affronted. "I did not start the altercation, madam."

"Fair enough." Maggie sighed and backed off a step.

Gentry took the opportunity to move forward several paces. "I couldn't help noticing the sign on your other wagon. About books. And, er, what appears to be a Ramage printing press in this wagon."

Maggie decided not to budge another step. She had a very strong suspicion that Gentry's words carried more meaning than he intended. How would a man like this know enough about presses to recognize theirs as a Ramage?

"Are you in the trade yourself, Mr. Gentry?"

"Peripherally, just peripherally. You don't see many Ramages heading West. You don't even see many back in the States."

"I'm not an expert. You'd have to take up that subject with my husband."

"Perhaps I shall."

He moved closer. Maggie could feel the warmth of his body and smell the strong male scent about him. Not like Johnny, or even Red Eagle. This man's scent seemed compounded of bay rum and heat. A primal smell. Warning bells went off in her brain. Maggie took a stumbling step backwards.

His hand shot out to steady her. "What is a woman like you doing on this journey? You belong in finer places."

"I could ask the same of yourself," she spat back as she

loosed her arm from his grip. "We have predators enough already."

He laughed, and the sound was hard and sharp. "You would make a fine addition to my collection, my dear. My collection of precious things. I will leave you now, as duty calls. But I will return for you when the moment is ripe."

Flabbergasted, Maggie could think of no retort. She only watched as Gentry returned to his own territory.

That evening before dinner, Maggie was dutifully reporting to her husband most of what had occurred during her noon meeting with Gentry, when Jamie appeared with a smirk on his face and strawberry jam on his cheeks.

She stopped in mid-sentence and frowned. "Have you been begging sweets from the other train?"

"No, ma'am. I never would beg." He grinned to himself. Standing around looking hungry and hopeful wasn't the same as outright begging, no way. Besides, those people had so much of everything. It seemed a shame not to help share it.

"Where did you get the jam, then, young man?"

"Answer your mother, boy!"

Jamie's eyes skittered nervously to his father. He was still in a pretty bad way. Looked like trouble for sure. Jamie tried to remember the jam's sweetness for one more forbidden second. "Mr. Gentry. He was ever so polite about it. I didn't ask for it at all, truly! I was just walking around admiring his horses, and he comes up to me with this *huge* jar of jam and a spoon. He fills that spoon up right full and hands it to me, then starts in asking questions."

Johnny felt for his bruised cheek. "What kind of questions, Jamie?"

The boy stretched his tongue out as far as it would reach to get to some more of that leftover jam. "Oh, nothing special. Just about your printing trade, and wherever had we got such a fine press? Stuff like that."

"And what did you tell him?" Johnny's voice was too calm, like the summer prairie just before a thunderstorm.

"I told him to ask you, Pa, and the stinker pulls back the spoon afore I could dig in after some more!"

"Jamie! Watch your tongue!"

Jamie looked at his mother. He judged she wasn't really that angry. Then he looked at his father. Pa had let out his pent-up breath and was smiling. For the first time that day, as near as Jamie could remember.

"You did well, son. Now go off and play till dinner. But try to keep some distance between yourself and the Donner people. They're not our kind of folks. Understand?"

"Yes, sir. I guess so. Our kind of folks would leave out the jam if they had enough, like he did."

For once, Maggie and Johnny were in agreement when Johnny commented softly, "Something is rotten in the state of Denmark."

ten

Johnny recovered from his hangover. His face began to look as if it might regain its former shape again. But he hadn't slept with his wife in days. Mulish herself, Maggie noted that even if he'd agreed in theory that the Donner people were not "their kind of folks," Johnny seemed to feel duty-bound to give his aid and assistance to that poor struggling widow, Annabelle Lorcum. The fact that she had a perfectly competent hired drover to assist her did not seem to register with either the woman or Johnny.

Johnny could not quite explain the phenomenon himself. Something kept drawing him in the Donner Party's direction. He told himself he was conducting exploratory investigations into Gentry's background. But all he could learn was that the man was a competent gambler and sharpshooter, and that he had traveled extensively in Europe and the States before choosing the path West. If Johnny generally ended up near Annabelle's wagon, if he occasionally accepted one of her precious tinned sweet biscuits, why that was just being neighborly.

Maggie took to retiring early with the children in the book wagon, leaving her husband alone with the tent. It was a wise decision in light of the reign of terror that descended nightly from voracious mosquitoes, but it did nothing to improve either of their states of mind. Johnny would wake up, itchy and cranky, longing for the balm of his wife's smile. When it was not forthcoming, he'd go in search of one that was.

The drought continued. Even the fine ladies of the Donner Party began to wilt. The wagons crossed and recrossed the swift currents of the Sweet Water and were hit with clouds of sand and dust that dimmed the sky and sage-covered hills and penetrated everything. Then they ran into bad water at an alkali marsh.

It was the noon break again, and the wet depression seemed very inviting. The emigrants loosed their stock, too late testing of the water themselves. And once emerged in the waters, the recalcitrant animals would not be chased away or even stampeded from their drinks, but when filled, lay down with pitiful groans and could not be moved.

The Stuarts' wagon had been to the rear of the line again—for once a saving grace. Johnny had not yet freed their oxen before worried friends came running back. He left the poor beasts yoked, struggling to reach the water they smelled, tongues lolling, breasts heaving.

The Donner group was hardest hit. They'd insisted on barreling ahead that morning, saying they hadn't officially signed on with the Chandler Party and couldn't be constrained by its rules. Even with this insult, Maggie could not help feeling sorry for the new party. Scores of oxen were lying bloated around the marsh, moaning piteously.

She glanced at her husband. He was focused beyond the disaster, off into the mile-long marsh before them. There was a curious expression on his face.

He turned to his son. "Jamie. Run get me the ax and a bucket like a good boy, please."

Jamie ran, and Johnny squished off through the depression, mud and corrosive waters up to his knees. Soon Jamie was back, chasing after his father through the swamp before Maggie could stop him.

She watched as Johnny chose a spot covered with a tuft of sod and sank his ax into it. He did this again and yet again, stooping to examine something. Maggie was beyond curiosity by this point, and she finally scooped up Charlotte in one arm, her skirts in the other, and waded in.

"What is it, Johnny?"

He flashed one of his old grins, too long absent from his face. "Come and see, Meg!"

He was holding what appeared to be a hunk of ice in his hands. How could that be? Maggie went closer. It *was* ice! She watched as he held it to his tongue and tasted of it.

"It's clean. Pure water, I'd judge."

"But how did you ever—"

"Coming back from the buffalo hunt, Jim Bridger talked about an ice slough. I figured we should be coming near any day." He slung the six-inch piece into the bucket. "It's as good as any you harvested back in Ohio on your father's farm. We should be able to dig enough to water the animals and give the children a treat."

Maggie turned to Jamie. "Run back and get the shovel, son. I intend to help."

The boy hesitated. "Couldn't I have a little piece of it now? I'm mighty hot already, and I could show it to the others, to prove what Pa found."

Maggie laughed, and Johnny cut off a fist-sized hunk. Jamie raced back, holding the sliver in his hand like the miracle it was.

Soon the entire area was being dug up by both parties. They mined for it in the worst heat of the day as if it were gold, not water they were after.

Johnny was a hero again. There was talk about putting Johnny Stuart forward as captain when Chandler finally

pulled his hat out of the ring. It was a fair certainty
Chandler was on the verge of doing this. And hadn't
Stuart shown imagination today, daring during the buf-
falo hunts, and bravery over that Indian business?

Maggie ignored the remarks she caught. It was easy to
be the hero for a day. But as soon as the ice melted in all
those buckets, the same folks would be complaining
again as they wiped their brows—castigating Johnny, or
anyone else at hand, for not coming up with another
miracle for their comfort.

Still, she was refreshed by the incident. Refreshed
enough to assay an attempt at making it all up with
Johnny. Cutting up little chunks of ice for the baby to
suck on and play with, Maggie glanced around to where
her husband was tending their oxen. Her mouth was
forming into a smile to welcome him back into the fold
when Annabelle Lorcum sashayed into view, wringing
her petite, lily-white hands.

Without even a glance at his wife, Johnny dropped
everything to inspect the widow's ailing stock. Maggie
shut her lips into a thin line that was both unbecoming
and habit-forming.

On the far side of the marsh was good grass, and a final
halt was called for the day. It was necessary for the oxen
who had survived the bad piece of water. For the dozens
whose stomachs were yet swelling beneath the sun, there
was no longer any hope. For Maggie, too, hope was
wearing thin.

She was trying to grind together some pemmican in a
mortar when she received a rare visit from Ruth Winslow.
Maggie looked up in surprise. Her fingers dropped the

pestle that had been pulverizing jerky with an anger that would have destroyed any living thing beneath her hand.

"What is it?" Her question came out more aggressively than even Maggie had expected. She tried again as she saw Ruth flinch. "Excuse me. I fear my mind has not been harboring Christian thoughts of late."

The preacher's wife took a very tentative step forward. "If this is an ill-conceived moment—"

"No . . . no." Maggie sat back, her work forgotten. "I only feared for the continued existence of the entire male gender if they had been close by a minute past."

"It happens to you, too? I thought it was only myself. The . . . the anger that wells up, unwanted. I have tried so hard to fight it. Surely God could not countenance such feelings—"

"And why not? He knows everything! So I'm sure He understands how we might resent their swaggering, their womanizing. They act like lords of the earth! It's time women had some revenge!"

Ruth Winslow was taken aback at the thought, but not as much as Maggie might have expected. Perhaps such dark thoughts had a natural place in the barren landscape of earth they were currently traversing.

Ruth settled next to Maggie, anxious for a continuation of the most fascinating conversation she'd had in months. Her husband could not castigate her for this. This was *theology*, and she was but continuing his work.

"I cannot understand these sentiments from you, Mrs. Stuart. You, whose husband shoulders more of the communal work than any other man in both trains. Even now I saw him walking with your children. Had my husband been taking our children in hand, or some of the chores,

I would praise God whilst it lasted. Instead, he be in hiding, trying to meditate on the mysteries of the Donner Party—" She stumbled to a halt.

Maggie cut in quickly. "You've noticed something? Tell me, please!"

Ruth pulled back. "It's nothing. Just the Reverend's natural inclination to look for the bad before seeing the good. His feelings lie strongly with an Old Testament God."

"Meaning do unto others before they can do unto you? An eye for an eye?"

The preacher's wife sighed. "Something like that. I often wonder at the incongruity of it from a Christian minister's mouth. He would have fared better in the days of blood sacrifice atop a burning pyre. He'll not forget, and believes that no one else will, either."

Maggie's mind was churning at top speed. "Is that why he carries his hatred of the Mormons into his talks? Have they done something to you in the past?"

"It's not what they've done to us—" Suddenly Ruth Winslow was remembering herself again. "I've left something on the fire that must be looked after." She struggled to her feet.

Maggie caught her arm. "But what you came to talk about. It concerns the Donners, doesn't it?"

"It's nothing, only a feeling. My husband won't even come out of our wagon since they joined us, not until nightfall." She pulled herself free. "I really must go now."

Maggie watched the woman scurry back to her own fire like a frightened sparrow. She returned to her pemmican, but the anger was now replaced by more questions.

eleven

They finally made it to South Pass ten days after the Fourth of July. It had only been an additional hundred miles, but the trail had been on a steady incline, an almost imperceptible grade that the legs of oxen and travelers alike felt as a new strain. The Pass itself was unprepossessing, but its achievement was not. The cooler air at the top marked the dividing point of the continent—the halfway point of the trip, from whence waters would flow either to the Atlantic or the Pacific. It also marked the beginning of the Oregon country.

The descent was steeper. Oxen had to be held back, brakes applied to wagons. When they finally reached the other side, a halt was called near an unusual sight.

It was a fairly permanent camp of westerners, tents set up neatly, mules fattening in comfort. Maggie tried to ignore her natural curiosity and set in with her regular evening duties.   Before long, Sam and Gwen came around with offerings of sagebrush and scrubwood for the fire.

"It looks like more wormwood and sand to me," muttered Gwen of the new side of the continent.

Maggie shrugged and looked toward the grazing mules of the strangers. "Aren't you two off to see what that's all about? Everyone else is."

Sam sank down on a rock. "No need. It's that Hastings what Bridger warned us about. Already up on a soapbox preachin' about his *golden shore* to any what'll listen.

Ain't nobody talkin' me into anything but what I come for."

Maggie knit her brows. "Could there be truth in what he says?"

"Now don't you start up," chided Gwen. "The Donner people have already had too much to say. Then there's Josh Chandler, letting everything slide as if he's lost all interest in leading his train, and the Reverend Winslow, sneaking up behind Chandler's back, preaching for a new leader like he's just gotten tapped for the office by heaven." Gwen ground to a halt herself. "It seems as if everything's fallen apart since the Fourth."

Maggie inwardly agreed, but her mind focused on the preacher. "I thought Winslow had been keeping to his wagon."

"He was at that," threw in Sam. "He was even starting a rumor he might be down with the typhoid. Had some folks getting mighty tetchy on the subject. Ain't *nobody* from the Donner Party dare go near him or his family. Then he up and showed himself in public light this afternoon. It was a plumb quick cure. He looked right rested up, he did, with a glint in his eyes like he'd discovered the answer to all his problems. That's when he started in seekin' votes for himself."

Gwen had had enough of Winslow. "Even our suppers aren't like they used to be, especially with you and Johnny—" She stopped when Sam gave her a poke. Gwen threw him a dour look, but stubbornly continued. "I know I oughtn't to say anything. It's your own business, after all. But I do think Johnny's ready to be forgiven. And if you don't do it soon, he'll go looking for more permanent solace elsewhere. And it won't be among the party of the Chandler train! After all, if he'd only wanted to help widows, he could've taken a stronger interest in Grandma Richman a long time past. *She* hasn't got a hired drover."

Sam took Gwen's arm none too gently. "Come along, Gwen. We could do with a walk afore the meal."

She shook him off. "I've been walking all day, Sam. I haven't got another step in me. *You* take a walk."

Sam shrugged and left the ladies, but their privacy was not ordained, which was a modest comfort to Maggie. She really didn't need to have lectures on Annabelle Lorcum from her best friend.

Hazel came next, still looking poorly. Maggie put her husband's indiscretions out of her mind. "You're not showing yet. Do you feel anything?"

Hazel shook her head miserably. "Just some new aches. Kind of like shooting pains, right up my legs."

Maggie was worried. "Has there been any bleeding?"

"Not yet."

"Then it should be all right."

Hazel broke down into her handkerchief. "Oh, I surely hope so. With all this dust floating around, I can't but think the poor baby is strangling inside, gasping for air the way the girls do sometimes—"

Maggie placed a comforting hand on Hazel's shoulder. "Are you wearing a damp handkerchief around your nose and mouth during the worst of the dust storms?"

Hazel nodded yes.

"That's about all to be done. That, and drinking as much milk and water as you can manage. Why don't you go and try to sponge yourself down before suppertime. You can send baby Irene over with the girls. I'll look after her while you rest."

Hazel wiped her eyes and struggled up. "Thank you for your kindnesses, Maggie. I don't know what I'd do without the support of my friends."

Gwen shrugged as Hazel disappeared. "That woman's making a mighty big fuss over this pregnancy. Why, one of those women on the Donner train gave birth last night, and was around showing off the infant this morning."

"Then she was blessed, Gwen. You haven't had a child yet, or you'd know the feeling. Every woman takes to it differently. Hazel's not a beginner in the birthing business. If she says things don't feel right, she knows what she's talking about. I was terribly weak with Charlotte. I had to stay abed a few of the early months to hold her. Being pregnant's hard enough when you're settled down in one place. On the trail like this, I'd rather not think about it."

Neither of them had to, for the children, hordes of them, arrived. There were Maggie's own, the Krellers', and about a half dozen Richmans. They looked hot and tired and fractious, and their suppers wouldn't be ready for much longer than they were willing to wait.

Maggie sighed and started organizing. "All right. Line up for the water barrel, all of you!" She turned to Gwen. "You know where our dried apricots and prunes are stored. Bring out enough for two each, please. When children are hungry, they're hungry."

Soon the youngsters were queued up just like in a little school, splashing water over their fronts, stuffing fruit into their mouths. Maggie caught Jeremiah Winslow stealing into the group and snuck him an extra apricot. He deserved it after the ordeal with his father. She received a cherubic smile for her efforts.

Refreshed, the youngsters were sent to admire Lansford Hastings's mules. All except the babies. Mules and toddlers didn't go well together. Maggie tethered Charlotte and Irene to each other with a rope attached to the nearest wagon and gave them Charlotte's soft dolls to chew on so they wouldn't be tempted to stuff too much sand into their mouths.

Maggie finally turned her attention back to Gwen and the dinner. "You were saying?"

Gwen laughed. "Sure you didn't run an orphanage back East? Irish and I were in one after our parents died. But only for a year, thank God. They didn't have any dried apricots and they didn't have any smiles, but the lines were always there."

Maggie was surprised. "I thought you said you'd raised Irish yourself. How did you get out of the orphanage?"

Gwen grinned mischievously. "We escaped. We planned it all out together. Irish hated the place even more than I. One night we just snuck out of our beds and started walking."

"And they didn't go after you?"

Gwen shrugged. "They may have tried. But not too hard. There wasn't any dearth of orphans, so I guess they didn't really need us. That's when I got myself apprenticed to a seamstress, and Irish to a potter. When we'd saved up enough coins, we got our own room in a tenement and set up housekeeping. The rooms got bigger over the years, but I wasn't sorry to leave the smell of boiled cabbage behind when Irish got it into his head to change it all and leave."

Gwen peeked into the pot Maggie was stirring. "This

must be the first time in months I actually wish I could smell boiled cabbage cooking again."

"I've been remembering the spare ribs and noodles we used to eat in our Cincinnati boarding house, Gwen. You could get all the ribs you wanted—free for the taking—from the slaughter houses. And potatoes and sauerkraut were cheap. Incredibly cheap, thinking about it."

"Don't forget the dill pickles," added a strong, low voice.

They looked up. Johnny was back from who knew where. Hastings's camp? Annabelle's lair?

He threw an armload of sagebrush near the fire and squatted next to Maggie, one hand held behind his back. "Since I obviously cannot have a pickle, why don't you describe what culinary delight is in store for us tonight?"

"Cornmeal mush. Sprinkled with jerky and fried with the last of our buffalo lard."

"Imaginative."

"I thought so." Then she closed her mouth. They weren't speaking, after all.

Johnny tried again. "Hastings gives a good talk. Almost good enough to put me off of Oregon. Certainly good enough to confuse many."

"More chin-high clover in California, Johnny?" Maggie couldn't resist.

"Maybe. But nothing like this." He pulled the hand from behind his back and presented his wife with a yellow cactus flower. It was frail, yet lovely, the fleeting, unexpected blossom of the desert.

She put out her hand to accept the offering, a small smile forming on her face, then pulled back. "It would go better with the widow's black hair, wouldn't it?"

Johnny growled in frustration and threw the flower into the fire. They both watched it shrivel into ashes. He got up. "I'm not sure what it is you're wanting from me, Meg. But I'm beginning to believe that, whatever it is, I can't be giving it."

Maggie, close to tears, half rose after him, then stopped. She looked toward Gwen, but her friend was backing away to safer territory. She'd already expressed herself, all too clearly, on the subject. Why was she doing this to herself? Why was she doing it to Johnny? Hadn't he proven his love for her too many times already? Hadn't he killed a man in defense of her honor? What *did* she want from him?

That was the problem. Maggie didn't know. *Lord, please help me, because I can't seem to help myself anymore.* Her life had become a confusion of sand and wind and hunger and hurt and crying babies. *Crying babies.*

Charlotte and Irene had tied themselves into knots with their rope tether. Maggie got up to untangle and comfort them.

They set off the next day for the Dry Sandy. Hastings had personally visited each campfire during the evening. The thin, youthfully blond man had a shifty look in his eyes, the look Maggie had seen before in snake-oil salesmen. He was leaving no stone unturned to promote his California route, emphasizing not only the warmth and luxury of his chosen land, but also the fact that it would cut off an entire month from the end of the trip.

The latter was more tempting than all the milk and honey he could describe. He seemed to have talked the

Donner Party into his scheme, and promised everyone he'd stick around the Pass a week or two longer. He'd catch up with the two groups at Fort Bridger and personally guide the California-bound on his cutoff past the Great Salt Lake.

The Chandler Party was in a turmoil of conflicting opinions. It wasn't only over the California business, either. Some of the men were pushing for California now, it was true, but there was further contention about whether to go with the Sublette Cutoff when they came to the Parting of the Ways in a day or two. The cutoff saved fifty miles by going through the Little Colorado Desert and avoiding Fort Bridger. It also traversed fifty waterless miles of territory. Was it worth pushing the stock to save those extra miles?

Johnny had studied his own animals and pronounced a firm no. He couldn't have made that decision back in April. He'd known little about oxen then. Months on the trail had taught him well, made him an expert. Maggie may not have agreed with her husband on personal matters, but she fervently went along with this particular decision. Most of the other wives would have agreed, too, but few of them were given a say in the decision.

When Chandler was pressed for his opinion on the new options, he merely mumbled into his beard. His wife and younger daughters were suffering badly from the constant sand and swirling dust. Their weak lungs were worrying the man. He was ready and willing to give up his captaincy.

twelve

Electioneering began in earnest at the Parting of the Ways. The Donner Party had already made their decision, but its men came to yell suggestions and cajole the Chandler folks. It was entertainment, after all.

Maggie had several shocks that evening. The first was when she saw Winslow step onto the traces of his wagon, Bible in hand, to give a campaign speech for himself. She'd known he'd appointed himself to run—for reasons known only to himself—but she hadn't realized the man had built up such a staunch following. Where had her mind been lately?

The dark night sky was lit only by fires and a lantern hanging from the wagon near Winslow's face. The light thus flickering on his freshly shaven cheeks looked more like the fires of hell than heaven. Maggie shivered and pulled her shawl more closely around her shoulders. She was glad the children were tucked into their beds.

Winslow stared at the crowd before beginning his speech. He was well satisfied with the decision he'd made. It had taken him almost a week of solitude in the wagon to come up with the idea, but the Lord hadn't let him down. It was a perfect cover. He'd smelled something Mormon about the Donner train when it first pulled up at Independence Rock. He hadn't had the freedom to find the one person or persons responsible for that feeling but had grasped onto it, like a gospel truth. Whoever the Danites might be among them, they would never suspect someone willing to put his face before the public in this manner.

Completely satisfied, Winslow launched into his talk, carefully editing out any of the anti-Mormonisms that had peppered his former public appearances. His voice came full and rich from his throat. His years of practice, speaking to his flocks, would always serve him well. The voice was compelling. It was the words which gave pause.

Maggie tried to listen closely to the bits about Moses leading the Chosen People over the desert for forty years, but her attention was diverted by a jostling nearby in the crowd. Her eyes wandered to pick up Gentry elbowing his way close. She cringed. She'd avoided the man like the plague since their meeting on the day following the Fourth. Now he seemed to be seeking her out. She knew not whether he was truly in pursuit of her, like a more distasteful Red Eagle, or whether he was still searching for intelligence on their press, having failed in his attempts to bribe the information from an innocent child. She directed her eyes back to Winslow.

"'Brethren,' wrote St. Paul, 'if a man be overtaken in a fault, ye which are spiritual, restore such an one in the spirit of meekness.' Our camp has lost its heart and soul of late through such faults. Faults I pointed out back at Richman's grave—"

"Is he being taken in seriousness?" The voice was next to her, along with the scent of bay rum. Just imagine Johnny even considering packing bay rum to travel West.

Maggie could not help glancing at the gambler. "I fear so."

Gentry smiled wryly as Winslow continued. "Shall we dig our way deeper and deeper into the dust, both physically and metaphorically? I say no! As your leader I shall guide you—through the Lord—past no cutoffs of dubious origin and end. I shall take you only through the straight and narrow. To the very edge of the Columbia River! Be not misled by easy ways. There is no easy way in this life. Just as there is no easy way to heaven."

Gentry was murmuring again. "I note that your husband survived our introductions. He looked quite healthy when I saw him last . . . with the widow Lorcum."

Maggie didn't answer. How could she? The gambler was trying to further undermine her currently frail tie to Johnny. Things between them had been questionable since Red Eagle, but never as bad as since the so-called introduction to Gentry.

"Ought he not be at your side? The fair Annabelle is, after all, ensconced in her tent with a megrim."

Maggie tried to push farther into the crowd, away from Gentry. She did not need to hear about her husband's indiscretions from an almost total stranger, a stranger with morals more questionable than Johnny's. Johnny hadn't yet committed himself to the widow. He'd just gone where her own foul moods of late had pushed him.

If only she'd laughed over the incident the day after the Fourth! If only she'd taken his aching head into her arms and comforted him for his silly exuberance in over-celebrating the holiday! Perhaps she had blown the dance all out of proportion. Now it was almost too late.

"I can promise you my whole heart and soul and mind and strength in all our future endeavors," Winslow spoke on. "I can assure you, as well, that the Lord will be traveling with me and mine!"

The Reverend had finished almost before Maggie realized it. Secular politicking must be mellowing his oratory. And wonder of wonders, not a word cast in vain against the Mormons!

Before she knew it, Gentry was at her elbow again, sweeping her along with the crowd to another wagon, another speech. This time it was Al Jarboe, shoved up atop his traces good-naturedly by his cronies. Jarboe didn't waste many words. He just gave his reasons for wanting to take the cutoff tomorrow, ". . . and them that wants to follow will be welcome. And maybe, if we choose for California after that, it'd be all right, too." This was followed by a few loud cheers.

The crowd swung a final time. There were shouts of "Stuart! Stuart!" But still Maggie gasped when she saw Sam and Max hoist her own husband onto a third wagon.

Gentry noticed her reaction and put an arm protectively around her waist. She shrugged it off, but it returned, the fingers closing firmly. Maggie broke away violently, but remained shivering from the touch as she tried to focus on her husband. Johnny was grinning, running his fingers through that curly hair she so longed to touch once more.

Finally, he spoke. "It seems to me that politics is the only serious subject that men think themselves qualified to act upon without any previous education or instruction whatever. I guess maybe, in that way, I'm no different from any of you. I know what we're talking about is leading us the rest of the way to our new homes as best as possible. All of us could do it in a pinch. The politics part comes in being elected to the role of captain." He smiled. "Sounds mighty fine—*Captain*. Josh Chandler was elected captain way back in Independence at least ten years ago."

Laughter bubbled from the crowd.

"He did his duty well, as he saw fit, and I'm up here first to thank him for that." Johnny paused and waited for the burst of applause that followed. "I'm also here to apologize publicly for any treading I did on Captain Chandler's toes through general youthful high spirits." He sought out Chandler's face in the crowd and nodded at him. Chandler finally cracked a smile through his beard.

"It wasn't my fault I hit it off with Jim Bridger, any more than it was my fault I didn't personally take to Lansford Hastings and his California scheme a few days back at the Pass." Johnny stopped again to gather in all of his audience.

"Gentlemen, I've had a dream ever since I can remember. That dream has been taking me farther and farther West all of my life. For years, the dream was fed on books and words. More lately, it's been fed on buffalo steaks and cornmeal mush and—dare I say the dread word— *porridge*." He waited for the groans to subside before continuing. "But the dream has still only one word at the end of it, and that word is *not* California!"

A roar of appreciation enveloped Johnny. He was thoroughly enjoying himself. He scratched his chin and looked out on his audience like a child playing a guessing game. "Anybody care to venture what that one word might be?"

"Oregon!"

"Oregon!"

It was picked up and passed around like a chant until Johnny raised a hand to calm the crowd. "*Oregon.* The great Columbia River and the Willamette beyond. Cool rains that keep the grasses green for pasturage all the year round. Lands open for the taking. Lands that will suit us. I'm going to Oregon, and I'm going by the tried and true path. I've gotten a strong taste for adventuring lately, but it strikes me that you don't have to take cutoffs to find adventure on this journey. It'll be there when we least expect it. And I'll try to make decisions suited best to the time and place to get us through each new adventure. More than that I cannot promise."

Like the handsome sprite he seemed sometimes to be, Johnny bowed to the crowd and jumped down into it, disappearing in a sea of backslaps and cheers.

Maggie began to breathe again. She hadn't noticed when she'd stopped, but she seemed to need the cool night air badly just now. If she hadn't been in love with the man before, this would certainly have clinched it.

Johnny was youth, vigor, excitement. He was life to her. When would she have him back again? The gambler's recent attentions were forgotten, no more important than the constant dust which spread across the trail daily, obscuring clear vision. She wanted her Johnny.

Maggie headed back for her own wagons, not waiting for the voting which would soon begin. In her eyes there could be no contest. Not between Johnny and Winslow. Jarboe didn't count. He'd trot off on the cutoff tomorrow anyway, with three or four of his best friends following. They'd muddle along and maybe make it intact to where the two trails joined at the Bear River. Or maybe they wouldn't. She couldn't worry about all of them.

At her own fire, Maggie was about to put her hand on the book wagon door. A shape emerged from the darkness. It was the gambler again. She took the first step up. He stepped behind her.

"Your husband speaks well, as if he'd been born to it. It seems he can handle all the problems of our little world. All, that is, save his beautiful young wife."

Gentry swept her into his arms and captured her lips. He took them without asking, and let them go only when Maggie gathered together enough wits to give him a furious shove, toppling him unceremoniously into the dust.

She spoke her mind, her eyes flashing. "I realize our wagons shall be in close proximity to each other for at least another hundred miles, Mr. Gentry. After that, you'll be heading for California. I do not want to see you again between this time and that. Do I make myself clear?"

He was standing tall again, brushing the dust off his trousers. "I, too, shall make myself clear. You intrigued me from the start, and I shall have you yet."

"Never willingly, *Mr.* Gentry. I've met Indians with better manners than yours."

Maggie wrenched open the cabin door and called for Bacon. The coyote had grown large since his adoption, and he knew from whence his meals came. Maggie merely pointed at Gentry, and the animal leaped at him with a low growl, fangs exposed. Gentry reached for something within his frockcoat. Maggie feared it might be a gun.

"Bacon! Enough! Stay!"

The coyote stopped, but he fixed on his new enemy. Maggie knew he wouldn't forget.

Gentry gave a weak smile. It made him look a little older, a little more debauched than Maggie had remembered. Returning the pearl-handled pistol to his pocket, he disappeared into the night as a loud shout rent the air.

Maggie turned from the caravan steps toward the commotion. Someone was being hoisted onto the shoulders of the men, being paraded about. From this distance, and from the nature of the general hullabaloo, she surmised that her husband's head size would be expanding once more, this time to encompass the title of *Captain*. Fighting off mixed emotions of pride and sadness, Maggie shut herself into the wagon.

thirteen

The newly named Stuart Party was four wagons short because of Jarboe's defection for the Sublette Cutoff. It trailed the Donner group to the rear and took a week to make the next hundred miles to Fort Bridger. There, the Donners had high expectations of meeting with Hastings and being personally escorted the rest of the way to California.

Winslow kept to himself, appearing in public with a face grown even sterner from rejection. Or so it appeared to his fellows. Privately, the Reverend was congratulating himself for having made his point. Now considering himself almost home free, he tried to put his Mormon troubles behind him and concentrate on what even he could recognize as a potentially equal problem ahead of him. He'd made his bed and covered his tracks. Now he'd have to actually set his mind to saving the red-skinned heathen. The Whitman Mission would be before him sooner than he'd like.

As for the Stuarts themselves, young Jamie found himself leading oxen for longer periods and wandering less. His father's new duties kept him mounted on Dickens a fair part of each day—keeping the wagons together, giving advice and aid where needed. The family suppers were interrupted more often by emigrants worried about this or that. Before several nights had passed, Maggie began to understand why Chandler had so readily given up the dubious honor of his captaincy. Even if she'd wanted to make peace with her husband—and she had started to do so on several occasions, noting that he'd had neither the time nor the inclination to wander toward the widow's camp—each conversation was sure to be shortened by some new emergency.

The next occurred on the night they camped by Fort Bridger.

The grass and water were good where they lay by near the Green River, but the fort itself was a bigger disappointment than Laramie. It was nothing more than a collection of hovels surrounded by a ten-foot wall that seemed barely defensible. Somehow they'd all expected something more impressive from the hands of their hero, Bridger. The fort had little to offer in the way of amenities, either. There was only a blacksmith shop, a herd of questionable-looking goats, and a set of savage layabouts who appeared as if they'd welcome Jack Gentry and his talents with open arms.

Maggie took in the sight before her as she set about her usual supper preparations. Sam had bagged several jack-rabbits that day. Their stomachs would be full for once, but those goats in the distance—scraggly or not—were looking more and more appealing to her.

She was stirring a little flour into her stew to try to thicken the broth when Jamie ran up, distressed. "Ma! You gotta come quick! Miz Kreller's bad sick!"

Maggie paused only to scoop up her daughter and run to Gwen's wagon. Gwen was sitting on the backboard, her seamstress pad hung over her neck, giving her already ample bosom a puffy, pin-cushion effect. Her mouth was filled with needles.

Maggie plunked Charlotte down next to her. "You're in charge of the baby and the meal. Johnny's nowhere about, and Hazel's sick."

Before Gwen could clear her mouth to voice either protest or concern, Maggie had flown.

At the Krellers' wagon, she found the children milling about anxiously. She took one look at Hazel writhing on a bedroll within and took over. "Jamie and Matty, front and center!"

The two children—her own and the eldest Kreller—jumped to stand before her.

"I'm giving you a very important job. You must run to the fort together and look for your fathers. Tell them they're needed back here at once." Before she'd finished, they'd begun running. She shouted after them. "Hold each other's hands! And don't talk to any strangers!"

Maggie searched for Hilda next. The child was waiting, eyes large with fear. "Take little Irene to Gwen. You know Gwen? The lady with the yellow hair?" Hilda nodded. "Next, run and get Grandma Richman. Can you do all of that?"

"Yes, ma'am."

"Go!"

Maggie poked at the fire Hazel had started and put on some water to boil. Finally she was ready to enter the wagon, a damp cloth in her hand.

Hazel was groaning, her eyes vacant with pain. Maggie opened her dress, bathed away some of the sweat, and held her friend's hand. She was very small and frail lying so before her, her dark hair swept about in the disarray of fever. Maggie knew she'd have to undress Hazel, but was praying Grandma Richman would come to give her some support.

In answer to her prayer, a strong voice came through the wagon opening. "How's she doin'?"

"Not as well as I'd like."

"Shove yourself over, dearie, and give me some room for a look." Grandma bustled in and wasted no time. In a moment she was making her prognosis. "*Tsk*. Don't look good a tall. The baby's a goner for sure. Bring me that hot water and a pan. Gotta mop up some of this blood afore I see about savin' Hazel."

It seemed forever before Max and Johnny arrived. By then, Grandma had taken over completely. As she put it, there "weren't enough room in this here wagon for no sightseers."

Maggie made coffee for the men, serving it first to the distracted Max. He was pacing, even his pipe offering no solace. Every few minutes he'd poke his head into the wagon after one of Hazel's more prominent shrieks. He'd shake his head and renew his pacing.

Finally he paused before Johnny, oblivious of Maggie's presence. "I can live without the baby. Even if it *was* a boy." Pain etched grooves into his comfortable face. "Grandma said it was a boy—" His feet circled the fire yet again. "I can learn to live without the baby. But I can't learn to live without Hazel. We been together since we was just children, seems like. She don't look like much to most folks, but she's part of me . . . a good woman. A good mother." He pulled out his tobacco pouch again and wandered into the night.

Johnny faced Maggie across the cookfire. Their eyes met for an eternity. Suddenly he tossed down his cup and went to her. His arms reached out and she entered into them willingly. "God help me. Help *us*. I've been a complete fool," he whispered hoarsely. "Can you ever forgive me, Meg, love?"

"It takes two to keep a fight going. I'm every bit as much to blame."

"May we start over again? *Please*? It may not be as comfortable for a while. Not with this captaincy chore hanging over me. Seems like I'm never with you when I want to be anymore. And I did want to be. But you looked so angry all the time, or sad. The sadness was even worse, knowing I'd brought it on."

Maggie burrowed deeply into his embrace. "If I know you're with me in your heart, I can survive anything, Johnny. I just wasn't sure anymore. . . . And I can help you, Johnny, with your new work. I should have told you that sooner. How proud I was when you were elected, and I never told you—"

Maggie was crying softly into his shoulder. They were gentle tears, pent up from her worry over Hazel. She would not let them become vicious, a leftover from the weeks of friction between herself and Johnny. Just healing. His arms tightened around her and they stood there, together again as the night darkened around their vigil.

Grandma's voice parted them. "Fetch Gwen and her needles and thread. Fast!"

Maggie looked fearfully into Johnny's eyes and bolted. She met a strange sight at their campfire. Sam had a sleeping Charlotte tucked up in his arms, Irish next to him whispering inanities to his own little armful—baby Irene. Jamie was curled up with Matty and Hilda on the buffalo robe by the fire, Bacon protectively at their feet.

"Where's Gwen?"

"Taking a little rest. How's Hazel?"

"Not good." Maggie ran again to find Gwen, to shake her awake.

Gwen opened her eyes. "What is it?"

"We need your sewing things and your skill . . . at once!"

"But—"

"No buts. You've got to stitch up Hazel."

Maggie could see Gwen blanch even through the darkness. But she got up, straightened her skirts, grabbed for her sewing bag, and followed Maggie.

Maggie watched with the men as Gwen hesitated by the wagon. Visibly she pulled herself together and hoisted herself up to perform her chore of mercy. They could hear Grandma giving orders, could see the women silhouetted against the canvas by the lantern within.

"It's no trouble, child. I done it many times afore, but my eyesight's not what it used to be. And it's firm, steady hands what are called for. She lost some of her insides with the baby, and I had to open her up to get it all out. No savin' her otherwise."

Gwen was mumbling incoherently. It sounded like a plea to heaven. But the shadow of her hands through the cloth carefully began threading an invisible needle. Maggie turned away. She could not watch more. Her own hands shaking, she went to rattle the coffeepot and fill it again. Incapable of doing anything else, she knelt down beside Johnny and rested her head on his chest to wait.

Gwen lingered after her work, drinking a cup of coffee with the others, in silence. Fingers that had acted so firmly professional within the wagon were trembling uncontrollably. Maggie shooed her off to put the babies to bed.

It must have been two in the morning when Grandma finally eased her tired bones out of the wagon. "It's time to see if my lot have killed themselves off yet," murmured Grandma.

"Johnny checked on them thrice. They're asleep now."

Grandma gave him a thankful nod. She turned to Max, whose muscles were strained taut, awaiting the verdict. "If we don't get no more blood, and she can rest easy for a while, no worries or interruptions, she might make it."

Max swallowed a sob. "I'll never be able to thank you, Grandma."

"Don't be givin' me no thanks yet. Send your prayers straight up to the Almighty." She swiveled around. "*Captain* Stuart, seems to me as how the stock could use a day of rest tomorrow."

"You took the words right out of my mouth, Grandma. And the folks up at the fort made mention of a little game hereabouts. I think it's high time this party brought in some meat for the next leg of the trip."

"Good. My younguns are startin' to look like sticks. Some rich broth be just what Hazel needs, too." She confronted Max a final time. "*If* she lives, Hazel won't be makin' any more babies for you. Thank the Lord you got your fine girls already, and don't be sorrowin' your mind for any more. And *if* she lives, she won't be in no mood for any night visitations for at least six weeks. Do I make myself clear?"

Max nodded dumbly.

Grandma waved her arms at all of them. "Go on, git! Off to bed with you. You can't be doin' no more now. Be needin' your strength for the new day."

They followed her orders.

Hazel was still alive the next morning. Weak, but alive. Max took no chances on the luck of the hunting party that set off early, but went to the fort and bartered for a goat. He brought one back, and presented it, still warm, to Maggie.

"I know I shouldn't be asking for more favors, but I was hoping you'd cook some good soup for Hazel."

Maggie had had next to no sleep in the remaining hours before the dawn. Life had seemed too precious a commodity to be wasted on that. Instead, she and Johnny had made up their differences in their tent. There had been more grace and tenderness than on their wedding night. Maggie may have been exhausted in body, but she was soaring in spirit.

"Max Kreller, don't you ever come begging to me. You and Hazel took over for us during our Indian troubles. You know I'm just returning what's due. And it's not out of duty, either, but love. You need something, ask!" She hauled out her soup kettle and took a second look at the goat. "But if you'd be kind enough to skin the creature for me, I'd be much obliged."

Max managed a small smile and proceeded with the butchering. Maggie sent the children out in search of wild onions and herbs, and before noon, she was spooning broth into her friend. The remainder of the day passed in smoking the largest part of the goat's meat, looking after two sets of children, and getting Gwen to help in doing the Kreller laundry, along with their own.

Contented hunters returned near sundown. They'd cornered a lone buffalo, lost from its herd, and four deer. They also brought tales of seeing a herd of wild horses, but they hadn't the time to pursue them.

There was plenty of meat at the fires that night, and the stock had rested well and grazed to their content during the day. Much as he desired it, Johnny as captain could find no further excuses to prolong their stay at Bridger. The bulk of the party was anxious to be moving on, and Hazel would have to take her chances by moving with them. The sickness of one member of the group could not take priority over the purpose of their journey.

They pulled out in the morning, leaving the Donner Party behind them to wait for Hastings. Maggie was not sorry to see the last of them. The widow Annabelle would have to start practicing her wiles on another man. And Jack Gentry, for all of his threats, would make no more approaches to Maggie, no further inquiries into the antecedents of their printing press. The last she heard, Gentry was happily bilking the fort's residents of their earthly resources in a nonstop card game.

fourteen

Jack Gentry was, indeed, practicing one of his many marketable skills. The quickness of his eyes and fingers, as well as the glibness of his tongue, were only some of the many talents that had endeared him to Brigham Young.

He sat now in a dark and smoky hovel at Fort Bridger, at a table pockmarked by the inscriptions of many knives, surrounded by the dregs of humanity. He was dealing out another poker hand. The action was natural, requiring no thought, leaving his mind free to roam through the many levels of his current mission. He'd learned of Joseph Smith's assassination while he was in England, seeking recruits for the new city of Nauvoo. He'd been one of the few to see the beauty of the disaster. Ridding the organization of Joseph Smith and his mostly absurd prophecies left the field open to the strongest—and Gentry's good friend and confidant, Brigham Young, had been quick to clear out the remaining rubbish and assume power. Gentry, under another name, had been recalled to assist at this task. After the structure of Mormonism had been assured, he was freed for the next chore. Revenge. As little as he privately felt about Smith, Gentry understood the necessity of revenge.

Catching the glint of white in a filthy shirtsleeve, Gentry's pearl-handled revolver took aim at the man across the table in a split second. "Show your hand, Carter."

Gulping, the skinny, sorry excuse for a human being spread his cards.

"Now, show the card up your sleeve."

Reluctantly, Carter pulled out the ace of spades.

"Wouldn't have helped with this hand at all, would it?" Gentry cocked his pistol. "Get out of my sight before I do you justice. There's many another man willing to take your place at this table."

Carter shoved himself out of his chair petulantly. Standing, he paused to reach for his winnings.

Gentry's pistol butt crashed onto his fingers. The sound of splintering bones filled the deathly stillness of the room. "That'll be my share now, Carter. Cheaters haven't got a right to the takings."

Carter slithered out of the room, favoring his injured hand and muttering to himself. His seat was immediately filled by another mountain man. Gentry called in the hand and redealt.

Yes. Revenge. First there had been the Carthage Greys to deal with. He and his fellow Danites had picked off several of the officers. Just enough to put the fear of the Mormon god into the local militia. Next, they'd done the same with a selection of local leaders, making sure to cover men from a three-county radius so word of Mormon rage would spread.

But the real perpetrators of the deed had gone scot-free. They'd just disappeared into thin air. Until this winter. Some said Gentry and his Danite brothers had done their job of spreading fear too well. Nearly the whole state of Illinois had gotten up in arms and told the Mormons they were no longer wanted. Gentry—along with Brigham Young—had known it was for the best.

They'd shepherd their flock so far that no one would ever interfere with them again.

The whole city of Nauvoo had taken to the ice of the Mississippi, trekking pitifully across it with their earthly belongings in handcarts. Only then had word come that one of the planners of Smith's assassination—the *intelligence* behind the deed—was fleeing West with the spring. Feelers had been out for over a year. It had finally paid off. Much as most folks hated the Mormons, there were always those willing to spy for a few coins, or a good word with Brigham Young. It was just human nature. You didn't have to be a Jack Mormon to have the temperament of a Judas.

Gentry paused to light another cigar, to deal yet another hand. He'd felt so strongly that his prey was in that other wagon train—the Chandler/Stuart train. It wasn't only the Ramage press. But the press had set him off. How had it turned up here, out of the waters of the Mississippi?

When extracting information from the Stuart woman and child had not panned out, he'd tried learning more from their neighbors. Pah! He threw down his hand in exasperation. They were but dumb farmers, the lot of them. No imagination. To them, the Ramage was just another tool. If it couldn't plow the land, they could care less.

Gentry tapped the ash from his cigar impatiently. He would bide his time in this slovenly place for a few more days. A party of his brother Angels would be rendezvousing with him shortly. They'd be coming up from their surveying work around the Great Salt Lake. Perhaps they'd have more intelligence on the subject. They had started out after he.

If Gentry's prey were, indeed, aboard the train pulling out this morning, it would be child's play to catch up with the perpetrator on his own superb mount. He'd not let Brigham down. There was a place of glory waiting for Jack Gentry, or for whomever he chose to call himself in the new Mormon state.

And maybe he'd just haul along that red-headed wench. She'd add spice to his life while waiting for his other wives to catch up. Gentry grinned to himself. Maybe Joe Smith hadn't been half bad at that. Celestial Marriage was surely the stroke of a genius.

fifteen

Five days later, where the Sublette Cutoff met the old Oregon Trail at the Bear River, the Stuart Party caught up with the Jarboe Party. Jarboe and his group were camped by the side of the river, much the worse for wear.

Johnny called a stop for the noon break, and everyone crowded around to hear Jarboe's tale, Maggie included. She searched for the always weary face of Jarboe's wife and couldn't find it, so settled Charlotte between her legs to listen.

Jarboe was unshaven and gaunt, his clothes in worse shape than their own. He stared at Johnny wistfully before beginning.

"It weren't no fun. Lost Simpson's wagon halfway through, and two of his oxen. Had to leave it and double up. Then my Effie come down with a heat sickness in the dry part. I buried her two days back." He scratched his chin and cleared his throat. "The younguns miss her bad."

He brought his eyes up to Johnny and Chandler hovering nearby. "Had no idea whatsoever what it were like to be in charge. Iffen you take my apology, I wish you'd consider takin' us all back. Simpson an' Smith an' Peterson, they all agree with me." He looked over a shoulder for his cronies' support and they nodded vigorously.

Johnny didn't hesitate. He shoved out his hand to clasp Jarboe's. "We're all in this together, Al. We promised to help each other back in Independence, didn't we?"

Jarboe's hand clung to his. "I'm only sorry we weren't there to comfort you when you buried your wife. You need any help with your children, you just ask."

Jarboe did not say thank you, but the relief shown in his eyes. Maggie picked up Charlotte and went to seek out the Jarboe children. All but one of them were well past the babying stage, but that little one might be in need of a motherly bosom. Al Jarboe just wasn't built the right way.

Hazel was going to make it. It wasn't easy for her to jounce around in the wagon, but with Maggie and Gwen taking charge of her children and her meals, she grew a little stronger each day. Max did as much as he could. He even weathered the incredulous looks of most of the men of the party when he took to slinging his youngest daughter on his back each morning. It was a growing experience for him, as Maggie learned with a smile when he complained at supper of an incredibly sore back from the weight of his Irene.

She couldn't resist joshing him. "And Hazel, small as she is, never fussed?"

"Never! But I'll say one thing. She'll not be carrying the child like that again on this trip!"

"Amen to that!"

As they moved farther West through land alternately arid and sage-strewn or looking like craters on the moon, Maggie began to feel more and more like Christian in *The Pilgrim's Progress*. She began to understand more fully the words from Deuteronomy: "Thy heaven that is over thy head shall be brass, and the earth that is under thee shall be iron." But she also learned that "as thy days, so shall thy strength be."

The dried bits of buffalo and deer meat were never filling, but the jerky gave a wiry energy to everyone's endeavors. What had to be done was done.

The emigrants found brief relief in the effervescent waters of Soda Springs, pausing long enough to steam meals in the hot waters, and mix grains of sugar with the cool sparkling waters of Beer Springs for refreshing drinks. There followed an even drier spell between the Bear and Portneuf rivers, and the brief respite of Fort Hall, before following the Snake River to the Blue Mountains.

At Fort Hall, Maggie was reminded by the pleasant gentleman in charge that it was but ten years since Narcissa Whitman had been the first white woman to grace the fort's tables and to complete the overland trail. As wife of Captain John Stuart, Maggie was also invited to a meal with the fort's officers. She luxuriated in the attentions of the men, too long without the comforts of civilized places and civilized women. She especially luxuriated in turnips and bread fried in buffalo grease. Had Narcissa Whitman eaten turnips here? And had the fort's garden looked as poorly in the August heat of 1836?

Maggie dwelt more and more upon Mrs. Whitman and the mission as they continued their journey. She knew the sacrifices already made by women in her own train. But these sacrifices had been made for the greater good of those who would survive the journey to the greener lands of opportunity beyond. How must it feel to be going West with the foreknowledge that one would settle forever just short of those opportunities, in the parched lands before the final mountains to the coast? How must it feel to dedicate one's entire being to a group of Indians who would prefer to be left alone?

Maggie still shuddered when she remembered her possible fate among the mud huts of the Pawnee village so far behind. They'd seen a few Flathead from a distance around Fort Hall, and had heard much of the feared Blackfeet in the vicinity, but the Whitmans had actually settled themselves smack in the midst of the Cayuse. The missionary sentiments that had fired Maggie at the start of the journey were now undergoing a radical change. Her faith had taken a licking. She wondered now about the wisdom of bringing the words of the Bible or anything else to the Indians of Oregon. The results might only mean grief for all concerned.

It was currently Maggie's studied opinion that the Indians should be left to their own devices. They had, after all, been thriving in their own ways for eons. She was not the first to admit, though, that a good piece of damage had already been done. One rarely saw an Indian who was not swathed in a trade blanket. And each of the forts they'd visited had featured tin saddlebags—shaped to drape over a horse's sides, shaped to carry quantities of the white man's liquor home to the Indian villages. The white man had already done his worst in offering "civilization" to his red brother. Could a handful of missionaries hope to undo this work with a few words from God?

The Blue Mountains brought new stresses and new reliefs. The rapid rises and descents took a horrible toll of wagons and stock alike. Unshod animals developed sore feet and hobbled in pain. More wagons were lost, tum-

bling like acrobats down mountain sides. Family trea-
sures were left along the way, wept over by the women to
whom they represented mothers, fathers, friends, and
relatives, never more to be seen in this lifetime.

But the mountains also brought berries—hawthorne,
gooseberry, and serviceberry. Such sweets soothed many
a frayed temper, particularly among the children. The
bears, though, were a complete surprise.

sixteen

They were nooning in a small hidden valley between ridges. Maggie and Jamie were halfway up the next mountain, foraging for more of the sweet hawthorne berries that were as large as cherries and tasted like mealy apples. Maggie had grand plans for making fritters out of them with the absolute last of the communal flour for that evening's supper. Johnny was back at camp with the baby, fussing with Sam over the recent inroads the mountains had made on their wagon axles.

"Over there, Ma. A whole big clump of them!"

"Good work, Jamie. There might be just enough to fill our sack! Careful on that sharp rock, son."

"You needn't worry about me, Ma. My feet are like iron now."

"Yes, and they'll nevermore fit into your boots from Independence. Not after the past months of going barefoot."

"Not to worry, Ma. They'll fit mighty nice into those moccasins you're finishing off for me. I can't hardly wait till it's cold enough to try 'em out."

"Never wish the winter upon us, young man. This September sky already has the look of snow about it, and we've a few more ridges to get over yet."

"Uh, Ma—"

"Find more berries, Jamie?"

Jamie was slowly backing away from the bushes, toward his mother, whose back was turned to him.

123

"Maaa—!"

Maggie straightened up and swiveled. Facing Jamie from the far side of the clump was a very large, brown bear, equally intent on getting its fill of berries. Jamie bumped into his mother and they both stood frozen, staring. The bear was no more than ten or twelve feet away, calmly ambling from one fruit to another, pausing to stuff each into its mouth. It was on all four feet, so it was hard to tell its precise size, but it looked *big*.

"Jam-ie!" Maggie's voice rose to a squeal, then descended to a whisper. "Jamie. Get your father and his gun. Run!"

The boy turned tail, and his mother followed, careful not to upset the bear with too much noise. She paused once to verify that the animal was still eating before speeding her steps.

Maggie skidded into camp in time to watch Johnny and Sam take off in the direction from which she'd just come. That they would shoot the animal was too much to hope for. The meat was badly needed. Surely the beast would have shuffled off by now to some hiding place. It had been so fat and sleek—so happily, almost sleepily munching for its winter nap. Maggie found herself torn between wanting it, and hoping it would escape. In a flash of recognition, she knew how Johnny had felt when he'd killed those first buffalo.

Maggie hauled a protesting Jamie back within the confines of the camp. She checked to make sure Charlotte was resting in her hammock. She studied the mountain several times during all of this. Finally she could stand it no longer. Instinctively grabbing her cooking knife, she hiked back up the ridge to find Johnny and Sam and the bear.

The first shot reached Maggie's ears when she was halfway to the berry bushes. She waited for a second, but it never came. Could it have been done so quickly? Maggie pushed ahead, ignoring the sudden stubbing of toes where her shoes had given out and her feet poked through worn leather.

When she came to the little cleft in the mountain, she stopped stock still. They'd shot the bear all right, but it had only been grazed. Now it was mad. Johnny and Sam were both backed up against a rocky wall, useless rifles at their feet. The bear was roaring at them, stumbling closer, favoring its right paw, but still intent on revenge. Both men had their hunting knives out, they and their weapons dwarfed by the eight-foot beast. Locked into their life-and-death drama, none of them saw or heard Maggie's approach.

Thoughts flew through her head. She ought to run for more men and guns. No. The trip would take too long. Johnny and Sam would be horribly mauled or dead by the time she could return with help.

Even as she considered these things, the bear's paws were raised, two-inch-long claws outstretched to rake his enemies. The hump of fur behind his thick neck bristled. He was awesome in his fury. Magnificent. The spell was broken when the animal uttered a cry from deep within its chest and lumbered forward for the kill.

Maggie did the only thing she could. Her tense limbs finally free again, she raced forward to thrust her knife into the behemoth's back. It was not easy. She struck as hard as she could, into tight muscle and bone. While she was struggling to pull the knife out for another thrust, the bear pivoted, loosing the weapon.

Maggie felt the beast's breath on her face. She smelled the berries it had eaten. She saw too closely the incredible size of its teeth. She looked on the hatred in its eyes. Yes, it was pure hatred, not the dumb bewilderment of a buffalo cow.

She quailed for a split second, then her courage tripled. No one, and especially not a vicious brute like this, would get the better of Margaret McDonald Stuart. Her hand on the knife was like rock. The bear's paw swung again, toward her.

"Johnny!!" Maggie ducked the swing, thrust upwards with the knife, and felt the hilt close in on rough, sticky fur. She was enveloped by a world of black as the bear embraced and fell upon her.

Maggie was suffocating. The entire weight of the world had descended upon her. She could feel nothing. No fingers. No toes. Nothing would move. She tried to cry out, but the words were muffled in her mouth. What was happening?

Slowly she remembered. The bear. The pleasant, innocently berry-munching bear. He'd gotten his revenge, after all. She tried for more breath, and slowly, very slowly, it came. She attempted lifting an eyelid. Light began to filter into her heavy cave. Next came sounds.

"Meg! Meg, love! Can you hear me?" It was Johnny.

"Tryin' to move the bear, Maggie. Feels heavy as a buffalo." That would be Sam.

Slowly, pieces of Maggie were released. A weight was removed from her chest, and she breathed easier. The lower half of her body was still trapped.

"Sam, Sam! I *know* you're stronger than that! We've got to free the rest of her. Dear God, if she's hurt badly—"

There was a huge grunt from Sam, and the bear rolled free. Maggie lay there, unmoving. Sam was sitting by her side, winded. Johnny knelt by her head and cradled it in his lap. Tears of worry and relief were streaming down his sunburned face. "It's over, Meg, love. The bear's dead. You killed it good and proper."

"Did I . . . do as well as a squaw, Johnny?"

"Better. Much better. It was a grizzly, Meg. A black or a brown would've run off. Grizzlies fight to the death."

"Was it really as big as it felt?"

"It must be near to nine hundred pounds. The skin will be yours, and the teeth, too. I'll make you a necklace."

Her face was wet from his tears as he rocked her. "Please try to move now, love. Tell me you can move." It was a plea straight from his heart.

Maggie smiled up at her Johnny. He did love her. Any fool could see that he truly loved her. She wanted very much to make him happy, to do what he asked. She sent a message from her head to get her body moving. The message must have gotten mixed up along the way. She was so tired . . . so dizzy. Johnny's face was moving about above her. There were two of him. Now three. How nice. There couldn't ever be too many Johnnies.

She blinked and tried to concentrate. What was she supposed to be doing? Yes. That was it. Move her body. Well, maybe just a little bit of it. Try an arm or a finger. Left hand or right? The decision was too complicated. Maggie blinked again, tried focusing once more on Johnny's three heads, and closed her eyes.

"Sam!"

Johnny clung to his wife in desperation. She was warm, she was breathing. He had seen the love for him in her eyes. But now she wasn't there. She'd just wandered off in her mind. Had she hit her head? His eyes searched the ground for rocks. There were too many of them. What would he do?

"Sam!"

"I be right here, Johnny." Sam was still breathing deeply, his gaze fixed on Maggie with a look beyond awe. "Sure didn't marry you no wilting violet. I never seen anything like her taking on that bear. It was scarier than you settin' atop that buffalo bull. Stared right into his eyes, she did. Like she was his equal."

Johnny cast aside the words of praise distractedly. "Maggie's equal to anyone or anything she wants to be equal to. She didn't need the bear to prove that. But, Sam, what will we do now?"

"For starters, get her back to camp. For seconds, call a break for the rest of the day. The animals is beat, and the grass is decent here. There's no telling 'bout the next side of the mountain. Then we'll come fetch Maggie's bear."

Grandma Richman worked over Maggie's entire body, limb by limb. Finished, she directed herself to the crowd surrounding Maggie's figure, prone upon a buffalo skin by the caravan.

"I can't rightly tell what's the problem. Don't seem to be nothin' broke. It could be she's just had the wind taken outen her, good and proper. It's best we let her rest till her senses return."

Johnny held his two children to him. He was bereft. It was worse than when Maggie had been abducted by Red

Eagle. That time he'd had somewhere to ride off to, something to rant over, someone to fight. Now he felt useless.

He should have been able to hold back that bear. At least, he and Sam—the two of them together. But his first shot had been bad, and Sam's gun had jammed. They should have called in the other men before they'd run off like that, half cocked. Yet they'd both known the food situation. They hadn't dared to take the time to get up a proper hunting party and chance losing the game. They'd been cornered, with no way out.

Charlotte chose this moment to speak her first word. "Ma-ma?"

She tried to pull away from her father's arms, to go to Maggie.

It was Jamie who comforted the baby. "It's gonna be all right, Charley. Mama's just tired. Gonna be all right." He looked into his father's eyes, begging him to make it so. Johnny held both children tighter.

Gentry rendezvoused with a dozen of his brother Danites just outside of Fort Bridger. It was a relief to be gone from that filthy place, to be free of the Donner Party at last. It was a relief to strip off his gambler's silks and dress like the man of action he was.

After the backslaps and general greetings, he wasted no time getting down to business. "What news have you?"

The eyes of his brother Avenging Angels shone out of faces browned to hard leather from the heat and sun. "It is as Brigham prophesied. We have found the place! A vast bowl of a valley next to the Great Salt Lake."

"With protecting desert on all sides."

"And water to be had for the digging. With irrigation, our people will prosper."

Gentry grinned. "I wish I could have been with you, but my mission was different. Do you bring me any other intelligence from the East?" He turned to the leader. "Come, Hoskins. Do we have a name yet for Smith's murderer?"

"We do, indeed."

"Don't keep me on tenterhooks, man. Out with it!"

Hoskins gave the information, carefully watching to see if it meant anything. "The Reverend Josiah Winslow."

Gentry cursed, balling one fist and striking his open palm. "The man gulled me good and proper! But I'll have him now. Who'll join me to the banks of the Columbia? Joseph Smith shall have his revenge at last!"

They all wanted to be in on the kill, but common sense held sway. Half the group headed back to give their surveying report to Brigham Young waiting in Iowa. Hoskins and five others joined Gentry to pick up the trail of the Stuart Party.

Maggie lay like the dead for three days. It was her turn to be jounced in a wagon over rough mountain trails. Irish took over her oxen while Gwen walked the Hardistys' own. A recovering Hazel and other neighbors pitched in with the children and the chores. The group closed ranks once more to lend a hand.

Through it all, Maggie lay, feeling nothing—a sleeping beauty straight out of one of Johnny's fairy-tale books. On the fourth day, the party made the precipitous descent that bypassed Ladd Canyon, emerging from the worst of the Blue Mountains.

Johnny stepped into the caravan during the nooning. He bent over his wife as he always did, to kiss her face, her lips.

This time her eyes fluttered open. "Johnny . . . the bear—"

His face broke into a smile like the rising sun. Lines newly etched upon his forehead eased away. "Thank the good Lord!"

"What is it?"

"You've been far away from us, Meg. Far away for too long. Can you move now? Can you feel?"

Maggie pushed herself up, almost bumping her head on the bunk above. "What is all this nonsense, Johnny? Of course I can . . . oh." She fell back again with a soft moan.

The lines returned to Johnny's brow. "What is it?"

"I feel so weak—"

"You've had nothing to eat for almost four days." He turned and shouted out the door. "Jamie! Jamie! Your mother's going to be fine! Get some soup from somebody. Anybody!"

Maggie rode for the last hundred miles to the Whitman Mission. All but the last day of it. She insisted on arriving there on her feet. After all, how could an invalid be expected to be maid of honor at the wedding of her best friend? Or to join in the festivities for the wedding of her best friend's brother?

Maggie's latest adventure had been the talk of the camp for days. Tales were circulated, embroidered, and recirculated about how she had taken her own bear with just guts and a bread knife. Maggie pooh-poohed it all. Still, the children flocked around her while she recuperated, bringing little presents of late berries, or one of the wild onions they knew she valued, begging for the story to be retold.

Most of the women wished in their hearts that they had not been so tied up with the children or the cooking to make the gesture themselves. Most of the men looked upon Maggie as a pariah. She was the same one who'd almost gotten them all into a fix over the Indians. She was the one who had blatantly egged her husband into fisti-cuffs with that no-account gambler.

Maggie Stuart was pure poison as far as the Jarboe and Smith and Simpson men were concerned, and many of the others, too. Luckily the trip was mostly over or there'd be no telling what mischief she'd be into next. Stringing her man around her little finger like that. Not that Stuart was a weakling where anything but his wife was concerned. That had been proven too many times already. He could've done in that bear without her inter-ference. Lord only knew what ideas that Maggie Stuart would be putting into the other women's heads. Women should be left to the cooking and the cleaning and the children—and pleasing their husbands, of course.

Johnny had been solicitous to a fault about Maggie since she'd come back to him. In his mind, she had returned from the dead. He'd already buried her so many times during those terrible three days. Had her buried and almost had the children raised alone in the new world. Raised by himself, without the love and support of this extraordinary woman.

He looked on Max and Hazel during this period with fresh eyes. He'd seen Max in agony. He'd seen his reprieve. Did he himself deserve the same reprieve? He prayed that it would be received, whether he was worthy or not. If he'd not been worthy enough before, he'd make it all up. In spades.

Johnny worked himself to a frazzle, worrying over these things while he went about his other duties. And when Maggie revived, he treated her like the most fragile of objects—the finest porcelain, the most delicate blown glass.

seventeen

The Whitman Mission spread out before the Stuart Party in the gentle afternoon sun of late September. The land was flat between a few bald, parched hills. The grasses were dry and waiting to be mown for hay. They flowed like a small sea past a browning garden, between a handful of buildings—unprotected by any stockade—down to a narrow river. Where the grasses stopped was a pent-up pond with ducks swimming upon it and a mill beside it. It seemed very idyllic.

The Reverend Winslow and his family had arrived at their new home. Winslow led the train in honor of the occasion. It had been Johnny's suggestion, as a parting gesture of grace and peace. Winslow had accepted the gesture in stride, his confidence returned, his leanness hammered to the consistency of unmalleable iron. His wife, Ruth, and the boys had not fared as well. The children were pasty and weak, and the woman had aged twenty years during the journey. But they'd made it with their Bibles intact.

The Stuart Party pulled up next to the water. Johnny left the wagons stretching in a long line, dug into the grooves carved out by those who had arrived during previous seasons. It was the first time in months their evening circle of security had not been needed.

In short order the small mission community was surrounding them—a flock of schoolchildren excused from their studies, assorted laborers and Indians, the Whitmans themselves.

"Welcome to Waiilatpu! We thank God that you arrived before the snows!"

Dr. Marcus Whitman was a tall, distinguished man. He wore a hat with its brim pulled down to keep the sun from his eyes. A strong, hooked nose presided over a full mustache and carefully trimmed chin beard. His shirtsleeves were rolled over bronzed, hardened arms as if he were no stranger to labor.

His wife, Narcissa, looked to be in her late thirties. The woman's light brown hair was parted in the center and pulled back in a twist from a face that was pleasant and attractively feminine, yet worn by some struggle of the soul. Still awed by this first white woman to cross the plains, Maggie instinctively took to her as she'd never taken to Ruth Winslow. But Maggie bided her time and held back, waiting for the Winslows to be properly welcomed. Only then did she come forward as the wife of Captain Stuart.

When she did, Narcissa Whitman took her hands in her own and made her welcome. "You must be so weary from the trip, and the last part still to go! I would hear everything of it. We receive company so seldom. Please make your children and your stock comfortable and join us for supper this night."

It was settled. Gwen and Irish buzzed about Johnny and Maggie as they made themselves presentable for the social event.

"The weddings, Maggie," pleaded Gwen. "Don't forget to raise our boon during the meal. Sam and I have waited so long and patiently. And Irish, too." She smiled affectionately at her younger brother. "Perhaps a little less patiently since he finally declared himself to sweet

Sue. It's too bad it happened right after your episode with the bear. You'd have loved the look of relief on Josh Chandler's face!"

"Mind your tongue, big sister. You're still not too old for me to whup!"

Gwen grinned mischievously at Irish as he wandered off in the direction of his Sue. The chatter resumed. "Tomorrow would be perfect. It will be another day as fine as this one. And it will be Sunday. I can freshen up my gown tonight."

Maggie couldn't resist teasing her friend. "Are you sure you'd rather not wait a little longer, Gwen? There's bound to be a priest in Oregon City."

"No!"

The answer was emphatic. Sam had been strung to the end of his tether, and Gwen had grown in the past months from the spinster who feared the touch of a man more than anything. "When we find a priest, we'll do it again. Sam says he doesn't mind. Besides, he's more used to preachers than I am, and Dr. Whitman does look like a godly man. I'm sure the Lord won't mind a slight diversion. It's the thought that counts, after all."

Maggie gave Gwen a hug. "For once I can't argue with you. But after tomorrow, Sam will have to take his chances with your cooking."

Gwen was crushed. "The evening meals, too, Maggie?"

Maggie laughed. "Of course not! You'll have to face him over breakfast, though. The suppers he'll learn to deal with on your own territory when we reach the Willamette Valley."

"Thank goodness!"

The Whitman dining room was austere, as were those parts of the main house through which Maggie and Johnny had been led. Whitewashed walls were unbroken, save for two curtainless windows. Roughhewn benches surrounded a long, plain board table, graced only with simple pottery plates and bowls of hot food.   After Dr. Whitman intoned the grace from the head of the table, Johnny jumped right in with questions about the last leg of their trip. "What are the chances of our taking that new Barlow Road I heard about at Fort Hall, sir?"

"I'm afraid it may be out of the question, Captain. My Indians brought me word that the first snows have already arrived in the higher mountains. It will be impassable until spring."

"Then it must be the river."

"Yes. But I'll send a few of my Cayuse along with you. They'll be useful for bargaining with the river guides at Fort Walla Walla. You realize, of course, that you'll have to break down your wagons and store everything aboard rafts?"

Johnny nodded.

"And the Chutes. You'll have to portage them. Although you should make it through the Cascades without too much trouble." He turned serious. "It is not a pleasure trip, I assure you."

"I did not anticipate that it would be, sir."

Johnny turned his attention to the food in front of him. Maggie knew he was thinking hard about this new information, else he'd certainly notice that he was shoving into his mouth the first potato they'd met in nearly six months. As for herself, she took a bite of hers delicately, and slowly relished its taste and texture. It actually had butter upon it, and a light sprinkling of freshly chopped green parsley. The Whitmans were faring better than she'd expected in this alien land.

Maggie glanced across the table to where the Winslows were seated. The Reverend Winslow was silent. Ruth Winslow was only picking at her food. Maybe her stomach couldn't accept the largess. Or maybe she was thinking about spending countless evenings to come among much the same company, discussing the day's advances and defeats with her fellow missionaries, never again to have a white-steepled church nestled in a green, thriving, civilized community.

Seated next to Ruth was the schoolmaster, a man named Gray. His long white beard gave him a dour appearance. It was not a St. Nicholas sort of beard, and his face had none of the compassion in it that his age might imply. Maggie bet he'd be a strict taskmaster. Filling in the benches were the children—the Winslows and the others.

She'd heard of the Sagers, all seven of them adopted by the Whitmans after their parents had died on the trail during the emigration of '44. The children were quiet, but seemed healthy and content. She could have brought Jamie and Charlotte to dinner, after all, instead of leaving them with Gwen. *Gwen*. The weddings.

Maggie turned to her host, sitting at the head of the table. "Would it be possible, Doctor Whitman, to perform several marriages tomorrow? We have friends who met upon the journey, and are much suited to each other—"

His face lit up and he smiled at his wife across the length of the table. "Surely the Lord is blessing us, my dear. There is nothing so pleasant as a wedding or a christening to bring joy into our lives."

"If it weren't for the wagon trains," his wife returned, "we'd have few enough of either."

Winslow spoke at last. "Surely you must be kept sufficiently busy with both amongst your flock here?"

Marcus Whitman stabbed his fork into a potato. "You will learn soon enough, Winslow, that the Cayuse have minds of their own."

"But the Mission Board—"

"The American Board of Missions is woefully behind in what is happening out here. On my trips home, I have begged them for more laborers. I asked for over two hundred. They sent me only yourself." He paused and reached for his water glass.

"Our mission at Waiilatpu has evolved differently than we expected. There are several outlying missions, of course, but here we have regrettably satisfied ourselves with looking after the bodies of the Cayuse who choose to come for medical attentions. And we educate our own and the children of the other missions, of course—along with a handful of converts. Then there are the annual trains. They've come to rely upon us as a stopping place, as you yourselves have done." He nodded to Johnny.

"We had fifty-five emigrants winter with us last year. They were too sick and weary to travel farther. We must labor long and hard during the summer months to fill the storehouse with food enough for these."

"You have accounts overdue, sir!" boomed Winslow. "Your mission is to bring the Word of God to the heathen!"

Dr. Whitman waved a hand wearily at Winslow. "The bodies must be mended before the minds can be reached,

Reverend. This you will learn soon enough. Like a mule, you can bring an Indian to the Water of Life, but you cannot force him to drink of it. Even their bodies are hard enough to cure. I cannot understand how it happens, but they die from ailments which are mere childhood illnesses to us . . . the measles or the mumps. And when such diseases do occur, they would rather take their ills to their witch doctors."

Whitman was tapping his fork now with ill-concealed impatience, about to add another grievance to his already long list. "With all we have tried to offer, the Cayuse absolutely refuse to learn our language. To this I say that stubbornness may go both ways. Until they learn our language, I refuse to learn theirs."

"How then do you communicate, may I ask?"

"Oh, a handful have come to us. You'll see them at tomorrow morning's service. They translate and perform other useful duties about the mission."

As if weary of the subject, Whitman turned again to Maggie. "It would be an honor and a pleasure to perform the nuptials tomorrow. Ask your friends to be prepared after the usual Sabbath services. About noon?"

Maggie nodded dumbly. She was still digesting what she had been privy to hear. Whitman seemed an intelligent man, yet he had chosen not to learn the language of his chosen flock in over ten years. It was beyond her ken. Had she herself been doomed to Red Eagle's village, she would already have made strides in becoming fluent in the Pawnee tongue. Certain barriers must be hurdled for the sake of understanding.

The meal ground on with Mrs. Whitman recounting her own trip West. Maggie could tell Johnny was itching to add their Pawnee and bear stories, but Maggie gave him a silent nudge. She intuited that her independent actions in these events would not be well received. Winslow would be gossiping about the Stuarts in his own good time. But by then Maggie would be long gone, her current reputation intact.

The evening was concluded with a reading from the Bible, and Maggie gratefully returned to her own world, thankful for once that her journey had not yet reached its end.

The Stuarts were dressing in the best finery Maggie could devise for the momentous weddings. Jamie insisted on wearing his newly finished buckskin vest over his good clean shirt. Maggie had arisen at dawn to stitch a last row of Indian beads on it, pondering all the while the incongruity of the gesture. By rights, she should be hating all things Indian. Yet she didn't. Flower Blossom and her family back in Independence returned to Maggie's mind for the first time in too long. She sighed. If only people could be accepted as just that—all members of the human race, all children of God.

Now Jamie was parading like a young peacock in the vest and his new moccasins. "Pa! Pa! Do I look fine?"

Johnny paused, straight-edged razor in hand, to admire the boy. "Never finer. A true citizen of the frontier. Incredibly motley."

"Motley is good, isn't it?"

"Son, out here motley is best. It's what we've got to offer—a little of everything, without the constraints of structured civilization. Improvisation."

"Oh. Well, then. Think I'll go show Matty and Jube."

Maggie giggled as she tried to force Charlotte into a dress she'd long since outgrown.

"What exactly is so funny, woman?"

"You could have just told him that he was handsome."

"He is handsome. And I'd rather have him dressed like that than in some fancy tailor-made duds. At least the boy has benefited from his experience. There's something to be learned and taken from each of our encounters, whether they be with the civilized or uncivilized. Even if you do still tremble at the passing of any new Indian." Johnny finished his shaving and wiped his face, giving Maggie a long assessing look.

"Yes, I know you still do, Meg, and I don't blame you. Still, after all this time, you haven't spoken ill of the race. You've accepted that their ways and ours are just plain different. You've settled this in your mind, the same as you settled that your grizzly had a right to keep living, but needed to be killed when our need was greater than his."

"God did give us dominion over the animals, Johnny," Maggie broke in softly, starting to take a brush to Charlotte's red curls. "But He never gave us the right to kill them without need. I was of mixed mind on that point when I climbed that mountain after you. But seeing you there, about to be attacked—"

Johnny nodded in complete understanding. With his back up against the side of that particular mountain, he'd known fear, real fear. But the fear had gotten worse when Meg had entered the scene. He tried to wipe the memory from his mind, tried to complete the thought he'd been working toward since their meal with the missionaries the night before. He gestured past their wagons to the buildings beyond.

"Whitman has stretched himself further than Josiah Winslow ever could, but he still hasn't learned his lesson well enough. His little settlement here is set out and run as if it were a village back East. He doesn't trust the Indians, yet won't put up security to prove he doesn't trust them. The man's living in a dream world with his bubble ready to be burst. Indians are a little bit like bears that way. They'll reach out for offered berries, beads, baubles . . . yet fight to the death to keep their freedom and their lives as they know it."

Maggie finished with her daughter and rose to give her husband a kiss on smooth cheeks. "Are you ready yourself, Professor Stuart? We'd best get started before we forget that the weddings are the purpose of this day." She caressed him again. "We can't really understand what the Whitmans are about after one night of conversation, dear . . . although I must admit that I, too, feel uncomfortable with the strange accommodations they've made."

Johnny hugged Maggie close. "I got on my high hat again, didn't I? It's all the *Captain* this and *Captain* that. It has me talking off the top of my head . . . the resident expert. Makes a fellow forget he's as mortal as the next man. . . . Oh, love, I can't wait till we reach Oregon City and become plain Johnny and Maggie Stuart again."

Maggie lingered in his arms a final moment. "Neither can I, Johnny." She eased out of his grasp to twirl before him. "And how is Mrs. Stuart looking this morning?"

"As lovely as the day. And it's a fine day for a wedding!"

The Stuart Party casually strolled toward the field that would be used for the Sabbath services. They were feeling festive. The weather was perfect, a boon on this day of rest. They were being given a respite from travel and a celebration at the same time. Everyone had on their Sunday best, the clothes carefully hoarded during the trip for an occasion such as this.

They were looking forward to the marriage feast that would follow, too. Sam and Irish had pitched in and bought one of the Whitmans' beef steers. It would be roasted on the spit during the course of the morning, to be ready for all after the "I do's" had been spoken.

Jamie was running up ahead. Maggie was following with Johnny, little Charlotte in the middle, holding a hand of each parent. Every other step she would giggle, cling extra tightly, and raise her feet from the ground to be suspended in mid-air. Laughing together at their daughter's enjoyment of this rare sport, the Stuarts bumped into Narcissa Whitman.

Maggie made apologies with smiling eyes that moved up the severe gray dress to the white face of the woman before them. "A fine Sabbath morning, Mrs. Whitman—" She stopped. The woman looked as if she'd seen a ghost. She was staring fixedly at Charlotte. "Is something wrong?"

Narcissa Whitman bent for the child, only to break her advance and rise again, head shaking. "Forgive me. Your child. She is so like my own was. Little Alice. So full of joy and life."

Maggie shooed Johnny and Charlotte ahead. "What happened?" She really didn't want to know. She already felt icy from the encounter.

"Drowned. Playing by the river. Our only child."

Maggie silently digested the information as Narcissa Whitman relived the experience yet again. She'd known there was more to this woman. She'd seen the sorrow hiding in her face.

"Joseph, one of our Indians, brought her up to me in his own arms. I was baking the bread. There were tears in his eyes as he laid Alice before me. She was a special child. Even the Indians loved her—"

"I'm so sorry—" What else could Maggie say? She *was* sorry. Just the relating of the story had caused her to grow cold, to lose the pleasure that had been in her heart.

"Marcus told me it was my punishment for having loved Alice too greatly, for having put her above God Himself. Maybe that is so, but there were tears in his eyes, too. We were both punished." Narcissa still stood before Maggie, in a trance.

She continued in a monotone. "It was a marriage of convenience. I had put my application before the Mission Board to come West. They refused me. It was too dangerous to consider sending an unmarried lady to the heathen. Then I heard Marcus speak, a friendship was formed . . . and in a year we were wed, and started West the week of our nuptials."

"Surely the Sager children have been a reprieve for you? Surely they were sent by God as a measure of forgiveness?" broke in Maggie. She herself could not believe that a merciful God would punish a mother for loving her only child. If that were so, there would be even less affection in a world sorely in need of more.

Narcissa Whitman slowly came out of her trance. "Yes. The Sagers . . . they're good children. But I hold myself back very firmly with them. I train them to obedience and learning carefully. It would not do to repeat my mistake." She looked around her hesitantly, noting the sunshine once more, and her husband standing before the group ready to preach. "I must go to my husband's side. He likes to have me at hand. He is so pleased to have a real flock to speak to today."

And the woman in gray was gone, leaving Maggie to search for her own little family, to thank God for their deliverance thus far, and to think how she might lavish more love upon them. There were too many already in this world grown distant and cold from fear of it. She understood this well. She'd already felt the very marrow in her bones growing chill when her foolish pride had kept her from Johnny for so long.

Gwen had done herself proud with her wedding dress, stitched in secrecy by candlelight. It was teal blue merino with fitted sleeves. The waist was narrow and came to a vee before ballooning out into a full, round skirt. There was a collar of lace around her neck, and bits of lace edging the sleeves from the underblouse, as well as a band of black velvet trimming the skirt. She'd made a charming bonnet of matching material. It lay flat over the crown of her head, with a ribbon tying it beneath her chin. Her blond hair was done up in spaniel curls for the occasion.

Gwen was truly a fetching sight as she stood proudly before Dr. Whitman, her bosom heaving slightly with exhilaration. Beside her, Sam Thayer looked like the cat who'd swallowed the mouse in an ancient, snug frock coat, a white shirt, and a cravat borrowed from Johnny.

Sue Chandler was no less lovely. She'd not had the foresight to bring along a wedding dress, or even the cloth for one, so she was married in her best yellow calico.

Irish Hardisty did not mind one bit. He did not even seem to notice.

Irish was a little under the weather from having celebrated his upcoming wedding late into the previous night with most of the men of the party. This morning he looked at the object of his affections with a mixed expression of pleasure and confusion. Had he really committed himself? Apparently so. Everyone was looking at him as though he had. And Papa Chandler would surely take his shotgun to him if he pulled out at this point. Irish assayed another glance at his bride to be. She was fresh, full of the bloom of youth and love. And he ought to get married sometime. Especially now that Gwen was deserting him. He wasn't at all used to fending for himself in the world.

For a final time Irish took in Sue's soft brown hair, pert nose, smiling lips, petite figure—the feminine characteristics which had egged him on. She hadn't Gwen's authority, of course, but she had time to grow into it. She would do. With a sigh, Irish turned back to Dr. Whitman. His headache would go away eventually, but he'd be married forever. He might as well put his heart into it.

Marcus Whitman stood before the two couples, beckoning them a step closer. A smile was on his lips as he read them their rights and duties as husband and wife. He gracefully led them through their vows, and concluded:

> *Rise up, my love, my fair one,*
> > *and come away.*
> *For, lo, the winter is past,*
> > *the rain is over and gone;*
> *The flowers appear on the earth;*
> > *the time of the singing of birds is come,*

> *and the voice of the turtle*
> *is heard in our land . . .*
> *Arise, my love, my fair one,*
> *and come away.*

"Let your joy together, your wisdom toward each other be as that of Solomon. Let your patience and steadfastness be that of Ruth. May you bring children into the new world to praise and love the Lord." He raised his hands in benediction over them and uttered, "Amen."

A general sigh of pleasure and satisfaction spread from the group surrounding the newlyweds. Few of the women's eyes were without tears. Even Grandma Richman snuffled into her voluminous handkerchief. Weddings were new beginnings, after all, and who could resist the fantasy of what new beginnings might bring? Hadn't all of those present left behind everything they treasured most for this very fantasy?

Maggie herself found tears unexpectedly streaming down her face. She was remembering her own wedding back in Ohio. She and Johnny had married in September, too. He'd gone off the summer before under orders from Maggie's father to grow and learn. He'd come back a full year later, after a week of autumn rains, bringing with him a preacher and the sun. Since then their joy had increased with the adoption of Jamie, the birth of their own daughter, and the lessons they'd learned on the trail. She and Johnny were still growing. Weddings were more than new beginnings. They also made people grateful for what they'd hung on to.

Maggie looked down at Charlotte. She'd been pulling at her mother's skirts, almost unnoticed, saying, "Mama, Ma-ma" over and over. She was alarmed by her mother's tears.

Maggie wiped her eyes, smiled at her daughter, and gave her a hug. "It's all right, darling. Mama is just crying because she's happy."

While the Stuart Party was celebrating the weddings, at ease in its joy and with the end of the journey in sight, Gentry and his brother Danites were not more than several hundred miles distant. They'd set up camp at a site that had harbored their prey not too long before.

Gentry was discussing their future strategy. "I say we take the cutoff around the Whitman Mission. It will shorten our trip. I intend to catch the train—and Winslow—before they make the choice of the Cascades or the river."

"We've gone over this before, Jack. I still think this Winslow might have been traveling purposely for the mission itself."

Gentry shook his head at Hoskins and leaned over him for another go at the coffeepot. "I say no. Winslow never would have been accepted as a candidate for captain of the train if he didn't intend to go the whole way. And if it's Indians he means to save, he'll find plenty of them beyond the Cascades. From what you've told me of him during his Carthage days, though, he's not the sort to go after the heathen. He probably means to set himself up in Oregon City with a sweet little white church like the one he ran off from. He left a rich parish, and you can't tithe the heathen, gentlemen."

A round of chuckles met Gentry as he tossed the dregs from his cup and rolled into his blankets. His muscles still ached from the hard ride of the past week. Only a few more days, and Winslow would be his! Gentry pulled the blankets more closely around his face as an image of Maggie Stuart's bright hair and flashing eyes pushed Winslow out of his head. That vixen would be a pleasant reward, indeed. A fitting dessert to top off his dinner of revenge. And just maybe he'd throw in her husband's Ramage press, too. Brigham would be pleased to find it waiting for him at the Great Salt Lake. The written word would be necessary to keep the newly arrived Mormon tribes in line with proper church teachings.

Gentry sighed with contentment. Soon it would all be his. But he'd keep the subject of the printing press to himself. No point in spreading the credit for what he now intended as his own special present to Brigham.

Before they departed the morning after the weddings, Maggie went up to the Whitmans' storehouse and squandered four whole dollars on ten pounds of potatoes. She clutched them to herself like a talisman all the way back to her wagons, turning only to gaze a final time on the brown clay brick of the mission buildings.

Dr. Whitman had been as good as his word. He was leading two Indian men down to their camp. They would be the guides to set them upon the Columbia safely. The potatoes would be her own little remembrance of the place, a sign that the fullness of the Willamette Valley so close, yet still so far, would soon enfold them all in its greenness, and succor them.

There were less than three hundred miles to go. Surely nothing could stop them from reaching their destination now.

eighteen

In two days the Stuart Party arrived at Fort Walla Walla. It was a stockaded outpost of the Hudson Bay Fur Trading Company and stood on a bare sandy plain where the Walla Walla joined the great Columbia River. Johnny went to see the Factor, the fort's head, immediately. He returned depressed. His group gathered around him to hear the news.

"They've a few bateaux available for purchase. But they are too dear, and not enough to handle all of us."

"What do we do then?"

"Any ideas on that, Johnny?"

Johnny stood considering his brood. He sorely wished he had only himself and his family to deal with at this point. For them, he'd trade nearly everything he had, buy a boat, and finish the trip. But selfishishness would get him nowhere. He must grapple with the problems of the entire group.

Johnny pointed at the low mountains around them. There were trees to be had there. Scraggly trees that had suffered through the vicissitudes of ages to grow to their present heights. Not many, but possibly enough.

"Sharpen your axes, men. Come morning we've got to harvest some of that wood and build us rafts. Tonight we have to meet with Whitman's Cayuse and the local tribes to work out a price for guiding us downriver."

"We come this far without help. I can't see paying good money to buy some at this point." Al Jarboe was whining

151

again, and he was joined by some of the others.

"Aye!"

"Answer that one, *Captain* Stuart!"

Maggie watched her husband sigh at Jarboe's stubbornness. That man just didn't seem to learn from his lessons. She knew what Johnny was thinking. She could almost hear it. The stock was done in. It hadn't another ten miles in it. The emigrants were exhausted and on the point of mutiny, the camaraderie of the wedding feast but two days before already forgotten with the last dry days on the road.

She watched Johnny hold up his hands for silence. "As to needing the guidance, there is no question in my mind. None. The local Indians have been born and bred on this river. They know its currents, it cascades, its hidden dangers. They stand ready to help us portage when necessary, and to use their experience in telling us when it *is* necessary." He waved at the vast mass of water within sight of their camp.

"Take a look at that river, men. It's not a shallow, placid Platte. It has the energy and the rains of the whole Northwest within it, and the mighty Pacific Ocean at its mouth. It is faster and deeper than anything we've yet encountered. The Factor tells me we'll need the Indians to float the empty rafts over the falls with ropes while we portage. And we'll need them to guide our stock along the river itself down to Fort Vancouver."

Johnny studied the river again. "The fact is, I'm thinking of sending the stock off ahead of us in a few days, after they're rested. These Indians know how to guide animals along paths next to the Columbia, single file, where we'd only lose them to the water."

"Ain't sendin' my stock off with no thievin' heathen."
Jarboe was at it again. "Not alone. Not after I brung 'em
this far."

"Are you volunteering to go with the guides, Al?"

Johnny's question stumped the older man. Finally he
just closed his mouth and sulked.

Johnny gathered in his audience again. "All right then.
If there aren't any other suggestions, we'll do it like I
said. Josh, Sam, Max, I'd appreciate it if you sat in with
me on the powwow tonight." He waited for the men to
nod agreement, then gestured for the company to be
dismissed.

Maggie watched her husband walk away from the
group, head high. He hadn't started out that way, but he
had become a leader of men. She was proud of him. She
felt so good, in fact, that she decided to sacrifice half of
her potatoes for the evening meal. Whitman's Indians
were even now fishing on the banks of the river, and she
sincerely hoped they'd bring offerings of something large
to her table. Maggie hummed to herself as she tended her
fire, made a bed of charcoal, and carefully buried the
potatoes in their skins beneath it.

Johnny came and stooped beside her. "How did that
go?"

Maggie beamed up at him. "Masterfully! You nipped
Jarboe's mutiny in the bud. I'm so proud of you!"

Johnny smiled, pleased with himself, pleased with his
wife. It was a fine feeling to know that *this* woman would
always give him support. Unequivocally. But not sense-
lessly. It was a very fine thing, indeed, to be appreciated
at his own home fire. He took her fingers in his, brushed
off the dust of ashes, and kissed them.

"What was that for?"

"I love you." And he was off again to continue his work.

Timber!

The hills around the fort rang with the sound of axes for the next few days. After the logs had been hauled down to the river's edge and the work of the horses and oxen was finished, Johnny sent the stock off with the Indians.

The emigrants watched their animals slowly wend their way around the great bend in the Columbia until they were out of sight. Would they ever see them again? Perhaps they should have traded a few to the people at the fort for money that had been offered. But if the stock did make it, they'd be better off to have hung on to it all when they reached the Willamette Valley. Stock meant more than a handful of mere coins out here. And these local Indians did seem friendlier than the Plains people they'd met before. Their animals might even reach Fort Vancouver before they did. With sighs the group finally returned to their construction.

The rafts were slung together crudely, just sturdy enough to get them downriver. Sam had been put in charge of the project, and he seemed to enjoy the opportunity to work with objects again, building.

Gwen flitted over to the riverbank many times each day to ooh and aah at the progress being made under her husband's supervision. Maggie had to laugh each time Gwen disappeared. Sam and Gwen were like two cooing doves, the "voice of the turtle" that Marcus Whitman had quoted from the *Song of Solomon* during their wedding ceremony.

"Marriage seems to agree with you, Gwen," Maggie began teasingly about a week past the wedding.

Gwen sat back from the cleanly laundered linens she was folding, a leg of Sam's huge union suit still clutched in one hand.

"He's so big, Maggie. You'd never think a man that big could be so gentle. To think that I lived in fear of men for so long. Such a lot of years wasted!"

"Not wasted, Gwen. Waiting. It just took you a little longer than some to find the right man, that's all."

Gwen finally released her grip with a sigh. "I could have let Irish go off on his own. There I'd be, stitching my heart out in Boston still, not knowing, never knowing, what could have been."

"But you didn't, Gwen, so you needn't waste time over regrets."

"It's not regretting I'm doing, Maggie. More like reveling!"

The rafts were finally finished. The loading came next. Wagons were hoisted aboard. Their wheels were removed and they were firmly roped down. Everything within the wagons had to be strapped down, too. Provisions must be made for safe cooking fires during the journey.

Finally there was nothing else to be done, nothing left to delay them from the river.

Other trains had come and gone, some laughing at the Stuart Party's fleet of crafts as they took to the dry mountains yet another time, preferring the dangers of what they knew to the water they did not. Others stayed, to hack again at the nearly denuded hills for rafts of their own. Johnny was unsure by this time whether he'd made the correct choice or not. Indecisiveness had never been one of his failings, however, so he carried on, chivying workmen from one project to another, spending time with each group to get his own hands dirty with the work. His worries he kept to himself. Survival of the river would be the final proof of the pudding.

On a gusty October morning, Johnny's party stuffed their tents and breakfast things aboard their rafts and stood a way off from them. They studied the river. They studied the wood of the rafts that would seem like so many toothpicks when pitted against the monstrous Columbia. Fear of the undertaking existed. And it was growing with each moment the emigrants stood glancing back and forth between their pitifully few possessions and the deep blue maw of the Columbia, forever etching its way farther into the dun-colored hills surrounding it.

Maggie and Johnny watched with the others, their hands clasped together. They both smelled the fear at the same time.

"*Now*, Johnny," Maggie whispered.

"I know. It must be now, or it will be never." He turned to face his fellow travelers. "Women and children board first, please. Ladies, remember what we discussed last night. All children under ten must be kept tethered. It doesn't matter if they can swim or not. We'll have no accidents from carelessness!"

He looked next to the men. "The gentlemen will kindly stay on firm ground until we launch each of the rafts. Then you must be quick about jumping aboard, or you're likely to be spending the next few days with the wrong woman!"

A few appreciative chuckles broke the tension before all swung into action. Each raft was almost fifty feet long and held two or three wagons, leaving precious little space for anything but basic attempts at navigation with the simply devised rudders to the rear of each craft. The final flotilla was made up of ten such rafts, and the Stuart family was to be in the last one, along with the Krellers and their wagon.

Maggie stood by on their own grounded raft while Johnny directed the launchings. Charlotte and Jamie were already strapped into their tethers. Charlotte's was long enough only for her to scramble about in the book wagon, while Jamie's had been lengthened to allow him access to the narrow decking outside. Charlotte was already squalling about being left stranded inside the cabin when she knew it was still daylight. Maggie ignored the outburst—her daughter was safe—and stood near Hazel, watching the rafts hit the water.

The men had set them all upon loose logs and were now rolling them, with great heaves, into the river. Each raft hit the surface with a stomach-jolting crash, stood almost upended for a split second, then slowly righted itself to float into the currents. Ropes were loosed from the shore and the rafts floated free. Each launching was as frightening as the first, and Maggie and Hazel unconsciously counted each occupant as they floated off, assuring themselves that none had yet fallen overboard.

"There go Irish and Sue, and Sam and Gwen."

"And Jarboe and Simpson seem to have gotten all their younguns aboard. Look! Isn't that Amaretta Jarboe? She can't be more than eight! Where's her tether?"

"I can't say, Hazel. You'd think Al Jarboe would have a little more sense, with his wife gone. Maybe Mabel Simpson will sort things out for him."

"Grandma Richman's raft has taken the lead! Will you look at all of those children poking out of her wagon!"

"She's floating with the Chandlers. They'll surely give her a hand."

And so it went until their own turn. Johnny and Max and a few local Indians pressed into service for the occasion remained. He and Max were so intensely focused on the launching that neither of them took in the growing sounds of galloping hoofbeats closing in on them.

"All set?" Johnny called to Maggie.

"As set as I'll ever be, Johnny. For heaven's sake, *do* it!"

"Not before you get into the cabin with Charley and Jamie and the pup. The baby's likely to get a nasty crack or two with no one to shield her from the settling."

"Merciful heavens, you're right!" Maggie flew to the book wagon. Thus, when the world turned upside down for a brief moment, she was not outside to be frightened by it. Instead, she was busily engaged in keeping her little ones from injury.

After the first great stomach-heaving lurch, and the settling that followed, Jamie broke away from her arms. "That was wonderful, Ma! Do we get to do more riding like that?"

"I sincerely hope not!"

Johnny was already at the door, grinning. "We've done it! We're on the river! Next stop, Fort Vancouver!"

He turned around to wave a cheerful goodbye to the watching Indians. The sight that met his eyes made him gasp loud enough to be heard over the rushing currents of the river. "I can't believe it!"

"What is it, Johnny?" Maggie poked her head out to look. "Oh, no!"

"It can't be, but it looks like that gambler from the Donner Party. Jack Gentry. And a half dozen others I don't recognize."

Johnny and Maggie stared with unbelieving eyes at the seven men who had vaulted from their heaving horses and now stood, intensely angry, watching the last of the Stuart Party's rafts slip from their grasp down the great Columbia River.

Gentry raised his fist into the heavens, and his shout was heard echoing after them. "The Danites shall have their revenge!"

Johnny's eyes met Maggie's. "Mormons! Gentry was a Mormon, after all!"

His glance turned instantly to his white-top, to his precious Ramage press. It was inconceivable that the Mormons would be pursuing him after all this time. Not across an entire continent for a printing press! Still—

Maggie's mind was working with other considerations. If Gentry pursued them down the river, and it was unrealistic to believe that he would not, after following them this far. . . . If he pursued them for whatever arcane revenge was on his mind, she knew without a doubt that she would be part of the man's program. She trembled. The fear was worse than during her Indian days. Jack Gentry was far more unprincipled than Red Eagle could ever be. Once in his clutches, she was lost. She grimaced to herself at another thought. Where was Winslow now that *his* destiny had finally appeared?

"Johnny! Gentry believes Winslow is still with us!"

"Of course! They must have bypassed the Whitman Mission to catch up with us! Winslow's ranting and worries weren't without foundation."

"What shall we do?"

He tried one of his old carefree smiles. "Carry on and enjoy our trip. It will take time for Gentry to organize transport to follow us." He laughed suddenly. "Even the devil himself will have a time of it, catching up with us now." His adventurer stance returned.

"You needn't relish it all quite so much, Johnny."

"The rest of the trip is out of our hands, Meg. And in God's. Fort Vancouver is soon enough to worry about Gentry and his men. They've got soldiers there to defend us." He grinned. "Are you intending to mope in here all day? Come out and see the sights! The river is amazing! We have no oxen to walk, the sky is the most gorgeous blue I've ever seen, and coming up around the bend is chimney rock and total security from the Danites."

"*I'm* coming, Pa! I want to see it *all*! What's a Danite? One of those rocky hills?" Jamie barreled into his father to be stopped by a firm hand.

"A Danite is a Mormon soldier, son."

"Does that mean they're wicked, like Reverend Winslow said?"

"No, Jamie. At least not all the Mormons. They're just people trying to worship God the way they see fit. If they're a little different from the rest of us, well, that's what America and the new territories are supposed to be about. Giving people a little room to think as they wish."

"Oh." Jamie digested the words and moved on to more critical concerns for a seven year old. "Well, then, may I go out now, please?"

"It's mighty wet out, son, and likely to get wetter as the logs take on water."

Nonplussed, Jamie bent over and pulled off his treasured moccasins, throwing them up on his bunk.

Johnny's restraining hand still held him. "I know you're tethered in, but that won't keep you from getting a very cold bath if you fall off the edge. It might take some doing to haul you back in if that happens. You be careful now, understand?"

Jamie nodded and was finally allowed out. Maggie strapped Charlotte into her hammock and followed. As she stepped down onto the rough deck, she gasped. Johnny hadn't been joking. The water was already ankle-deep over most of the deck.

She hiked up her skirts and turned to her husband. "Will it hold? We won't just continue to sink deeper into the river?"

"Not to worry. These are thick logs, and they've an incredible buoyancy. It's just going to be a damp trip." He took her arm and carefully led her to the front of the raft.

"Max took the first shift steering, so we can enjoy the trip for a while. Here's the bend now, where the Columbia turns from north and goes straight west to the Pacific. Isn't it magnificent? Look how dry the hills are around us. Not a speck of moisture, and here we are—"

"—as moist as you could please," finished Maggie. She was trying very hard to keep thoughts of Jack Gentry from her mind, to concentrate on the raft. There was no way Gentry could catch up with them before Fort

Vancouver. None. She kept repeating that thought to herself, like a litany.

She bent to wring out her wet skirts, finally turning to her husband, under control once more. "I do believe you planned this all strictly for the scenery. Try to tell me that isn't so, Johnny Stuart!"

He grinned, the heavy wind from the river sending his curls streaming out behind him. "What if I did? A journey such as ours should have a suitable ending. Suitably majestic."

Maggie smiled. "It is majestic. Pray God it remains only that."

nineteen

Gentry was back at Fort Walla Walla, arguing with the Factor over the price of his transport.

"Sir," he was told, "if you don't care for our price, you may take your horses over the mountains and negotiate with McLoughlin's people at Fort Vancouver."

"I won't need a boat at Fort Vancouver!"

"There you have it." The Factor gave a tight-lipped smile. He didn't care much for these hot-blooded men who had just swept down upon his domain, acting as though they owned the world. They would just have to learn about the facts of life in the Territory the hard way.

"It's all supply and demand, Mr. Gentry. I have the bateaux. If you choose to purchase one, you'll have to accept my price. I have a board of directors to report to in London each year."

Gentry had met others like this Factor in England. Uptight, unmoving tyrants, all of them. No wonder they'd lost the colonies. In the New World one had to adapt. He'd probably remain at this accursed outpost of sand for the rest of his career. "We'll meet your price. Which one may we have?"

The Factor pointed unerringly to a dilapidated hunk of wood sitting in solitude near the river.

"Sir, you test my patience!" roared Gentry.

"It is quite river-worthy, I assure you. It needs but a bit of caulking."

"What about those others?" Gentry pointed to several

163

boats that were obviously better maintained.

"They are the personal property of the Hudson Bay Company. For our own necessary transport." He was smiling now with a touch of superiority.

Gentry gave in. There wasn't much choice in the matter. "All right. How do we caulk a boat?"

"I'll be happy to sell you the tar and wadding for an extra fee."

Gentry grudgingly counted over the money he'd won at Fort Bridger. He'd get this Factor on his return. See if he didn't. He'd get a full return on his investment, and then some. He'd teach the Hudson Bay Company to deal more generously with Brigham Young's Danites in the future.

Gentry turned to his brothers. "We've lost enough time. Haul out the tar and let's get to work!"

By the next morning Maggie had found her sea legs, but the little Franklin stove in the book wagon had not. It sputtered and fumed as she tried to stoke it up. She'd spent a restless night, unused to actually covering miles while doing nothing. She'd tossed and turned with thoughts of being added to Gentry's harem. That's what his "collection of precious things" must be, after all. The man must be worse than a slaveholder to consider his wives as mere *things*.

Maggie gave her stove a futile shake. Adding to the claustrophobic feeling of the wagon was Jamie, already beginning to tire of the constrictions of the raft. Charlotte, understanding none of it, just wanted out. And then the rains had come. It had not rained for so long that at first the sounds on the roof had been a welcome novelty.

But now it was coming down hard, at an angle. Water was entering the little stovepipe atop their wagon, keeping the fire from catching. Her family needed something warm— at least some coffee—to keep the suddenly wintry, damp chills away. How quickly one could forget the excruciating heat of the past few months.

Maggie glanced out the tiny window by the stove. Jamie was monopolizing the other one. The vibrant blues and browns of yesterday were gone. The river was a vast, gray mass of sullen fury. The hills that closed in around them had grown larger, almost magically, overnight. They were cliffs now, with a scattering of spruce trees upon their ridges. The greens merged with the gray of the hills, the gray of the sky, the gray of the water.

The wagon shifted and creaked in its unaccustomed mooring, making Maggie grasp at anything to keep her footing. The dampness came at them from everywhere . . . from the floor, from the walls, spluttering out of her stove. Maggie was frightened. They'd come too far to succumb to a watery death. Yet she was not allowed to show her fright. The children would know instantly and then they would become frightened.

The only sensible member of the family was Bacon. He hadn't taken to this wet world, either. From the moment the raft had hit the river, he'd climbed into the nearest bunk and refused to be cajoled out of it. He just lay there, his head half hidden under a blanket, letting out occasional piteous howls. There was a sensible animal. He knew he'd been born to the land and he wasn't about to be talked into liking the water. Maggie wished she could join him under the blanket.

Johnny took to the new adventure like a buccaneer.

Maybe Maggie had been wrong about her assessment of her husband and the sea. Perhaps if the lands stopped, he'd take on the oceans, after all. It was another frightening thought that chilled Maggie more than the weather. Pray God there would be enough to keep Johnny busy on dry land at the end of this journey.

As if privy to her very thoughts, Johnny stormed into the cabin, wet and alive. "What? No coffee yet?" But he was smiling.

"You try fighting the stove in this weather, Johnny Stuart. I'd rather take on the rudder. Maybe even the Danites!"

He brushed her lips with his sparkling wet ones. "No matter. We'd just have to put it out again. We've come to our first portage!"

Maggie rushed back to the window to peer out. The water ahead was even choppier, and the rafts before them were all being directed to the south bank of the river.

"Is it the Chutes?"

"Yes! And a glorious sight it will be. A pity the weather isn't a bit more felicitous, though. We'll have to unload everything, remember, and carry it all for half a mile to the calmer water beyond."

Maggie squared her shoulders. What must be must be. At least they'd be getting sopping wet on land. And if they did it quickly, that would be one more natural defense between themselves and Gentry.

Soon they were heading for the banks themselves, their ropes being caught by the hands of many Indian helpers. On land again, Maggie and the children were shooed aside as the wagons were unstrapped and wheels set back in place. The Indians had a few horses with them, but it only dawned slowly on Maggie that they meant to haul the wagons with their own brute strength.

The portage took most of the day. The gray skies were growing even dimmer when the last raft was reloaded once more. Johnny oversaw the payment of their Indian assistants—the negotiated twist of tobacco for each man, and a few beads and trinkets—then looked at the skies and decided to camp on the shore till morning. His decision was accepted with great relief by all save his wife. Johnny gave her a shrug of understanding from across the camp, as if saying he'd rather not, but there was really no other choice. Fires were begun in the misty air.

Gentry and his men got their bateau into the water that same miserable morning. They'd worked half the night finishing repairs on the long, narrow craft by campfire light. The Factor had suggested they take an Indian guide with them to help negotiate various falls. Gentry had sneered. He was not about to fork over more of his dwindling supply of cash so that Mr. Superior Factor Samuel Saltworth could receive his cut. They'd manage just fine on their own.

Gentry took the forward position in the prow. He watched as the others maneuvered the craft into the river and jumped after it. They were on their way at last. With their extra speed they should make short work of catching their prey.

twenty

The Stuart Party came to their second portage at the Dalles mid-morning the following day. Here their passage through the river was hindered by several immense boulders which channeled the river between it with great fury. The detour was to be almost three miles. But, thankfully, the weather had improved, and Maggie and the other women found themselves with a holiday. They must only look after their children and walk the distance to where the rafts would be lowered by ropes over the falls to be once more reloaded.

The blessed sun was on her face once more, and Maggie examined with interest the occasional green of spruce about them, and the situation of the small missionary and Indian village on the cliffs above the Columbia. She began to see again, and the children helped.

"Ma! Look!"

"What is it, Jamie?"

"Over by those Indian shacks."

"The Whitmans said there would be any number of Indians here, Jamie. It's some sort of rendezvous point for them. For the fishing. There's supposed to be a small Methodist mission, too. Perhaps those buildings off towards the hills?"

"Never mind that, Ma," said Jamie impatiently. "There's something strange about these Indians. Look at their heads!"

Maggie looked. She felt almost impolite staring over

the distance. "Good gracious! They've been *flattened*!"
These must be more of the Flathead that they'd seen only
from a distance at Fort Hall.

"Were they born that way, Ma?"

"I hardly think so!"

"Could we walk over, please, to see?"

"How would you like people staring at your head?"

"Maybe if we took them a present? We've still got lots
of beads left."

Maggie was as intrigued as her son. And she knew
she'd need a diversion to keep herself from rushing to the
edge of the cliffs bordering the Columbia and peering
upstream like an idiot for signs of Gentry. He must be
well on his way in pursuit of them. Nothing could shake
that certainty from her mind. He wouldn't have stopped
to build a raft, though. He would have squandered Mormon funds on one of those expensive bateaux from the
fort.

"All right. Just one handful, though. There's no telling
what they'll be good for in the Willamette Valley."

Jamie raced off to their wagons. He returned in short
order with a bulging pocket and a broad smile. "I told Pa
what we were up to. He says to tell you to keep Charley
away from *flattening boards*. What did he mean?"

"I think we're about to find out."

Taking a child firmly in each hand, Maggie set off for
the grouping of hovels nearby. From all appearances,
these Flathead were even poorer than the Pawnee. But
there ought to be plenty of fish to keep them healthy.
Maybe they were camping here for the fish, and had
sturdier dwellings elsewhere. She hoped so. Her pace
slackened as she drew nearer.

Off behind the closest shack an Indian woman sat smoking fish over a fire. Her head had been flattened back to a point, leaving her with a long, sloping forehead liberally incised with symbolic tattoos. Beside her lay her papoose—arms, legs, and feet tightly strapped into a device that would have looked dangerous during the Inquisition.

Maggie groaned with pity. She suddenly realized what a flattening board was. Making an effort, Maggie smiled tremulously at the woman. The woman smiled back out of eyes heavy and dull. Maggie pointed at the baby. Charlotte began to whimper. Jamie dug into his pocket and presented his trove of beads, his own eyes wide.

The woman accepted their offering graciously. As if accustomed to the curiosity of white travelers, she began to show off her baby within its apparatus. She picked up the pressing board and slowly eased the tension, freeing the child from the upper and lower boards that were clamped at a tight angle over its head. She pointed out the soft squirrel skin tacked onto the board above the head position, as if that made everything all right. Next she removed her baby and pointed to its forming point with pride. The back of the head was purple and bruised from the unnatural strain. The baby let out a yelp of relief with the constraints removed, but seemed unsure how to move its limbs. They had been strapped down for too long.

Maggie blanched. She managed a quick "Thank you" and tore her children away from the show.

Jamie hung back, still fascinated. "Can't we watch her put the baby back in, Ma?"

"No!" Maggie hauled him along, almost running, until they had removed themselves from the Indians and their own people, too.

She finally collapsed upon a great black boulder near to the cliff's edge. Her breath came in heaves. Her stomach seemed ready to dispose of breakfast. Below them were the rocks of the Columbia. Indian men scampered over them, unafraid, beginning to ease the first of the rafts down the terrifying incline.

It would have been a fascinating show if Maggie hadn't had flattening boards behind her, and Gentry problems ahead. She assayed a quick glance upstream. Nothing yet.

The Flathead baby returned to haunt her. Would she ever understand the thinking of an Indian? She had learned from Flower Blossom—even from Red Eagle and his people—that Indians could love and see beauty in the world just as a white man could. It was just that an Indian's concept of beauty was often so *alien* to her own way of thinking.

Each tribe they'd encountered had interpreted the beautiful differently. Would it be the same with the ocean tribes they were sure to meet at the end of their journey? How would those tribes accept the new people coming, *her* people? Maggie's people were not just passing through, either. They meant to stay. They meant to use the same lands, the same resources as the native Indians themselves.

Would there truly be enough lands for all, or would she and Johnny and the others in their train be stealing from the red man, the same as earlier tribes encountered had tried to steal horses, even herself, from the emigrants' train? The thought was fresh. It was sobering. Where did morality begin and end? Where did one person's freedom begin and another's end?

Maggie pulled herself out of her reverie long enough to notice Charlotte tottering dangerously close to the precipice before them. Jamie was on his hands and knees nearby, absorbed in a carved fishing lure he'd found.

Maggie jumped up. "Charlotte!" She caught the child by one arm, and dragged her from the edge of the abyss, her heart in her mouth. She plunked her daughter down beside herself on the same boulder, out of harm's way. "Jamie! Can't you keep an eye out for your sister for one moment?"

The boy sat back on his haunches to study his mother. "You were right there, Ma. I didn't know you were still upset about those Flatheads. What was so awful about them, anyway? Pa said as how we all have different customs."

He stopped to hold out the bone implement in his hand for admiration. "Found a beauty, I did! Maybe I can try it out when we finally get to where we're going."

For once, Maggie ignored his offering. "You are not a mother, Jamie, and will never be a mother. Only a mother could truly understand the feeling of loathing that arises when she watches a human baby being deformed."

"It wasn't *that* bad, Ma."

"Did you see the look in the mother's eyes? As if most of her thinking powers had been squeezed out by the pressing? These people must be destroying their minds."

"Whooee." Jamie sauntered in front of her, his hand busily tucking the new treasure into a pocket. "You weren't even this upset when Pa rescued you from the Pawnee."

Maggie stared at her son, trying to think of something

more to say on the subject. He was acting unnaturally
grown up. Had his childhood been just another thing lost
along the trail over the past six months? She scratched at
the back of her neck absently.

"You're looking mighty strange, Ma." He came closer,
and dropped his worldly-wise attitude. "And your dress
has taken on a different hue, more gray-like than blue.
The cloth couldn't change colors from your upset, could
it?"

Maggie glanced at her skirts, then looked in horror at
Charlotte seated next to her. Her little dress was different,
too. Almost as if it were moving.

Jamie came closer still and reached out a hand. "Ma!
You're crawling all over!"

Maggie leapt up, and dragged the baby with her. In an
instant she realized she *was* crawling all over. She reached
out her hand, and found it covered with fleas. She turned
to inspect the boulder they'd been seated upon. It was
swarming with the creatures. Seeing clearly now, she
knew it was not a black rock at all.

Maggie jumped up and down in a mad dance, shaking
herself and her daughter. She forgot her own discomfort
and focused her attentions on Charlotte, who had begun
to scratch and cry. She ripped off the baby's clothing,
right down to her skin. Small wonder the little Flathead
infant had been lying in his press naked, his mother only
half-clothed beside him in this cool weather. At least they
could see the fleas that way.

What to do? She couldn't strip herself down to naked-
ness. It wouldn't do for the wife of the train's captain to
go running hysterically through even this tiny village.
But that was what she wanted to do with all of her might.

Maggie handed Charlotte to Jamie. She jiggled and shook till about ten percent of the new population had left her presence. It wasn't enough. She grabbed the baby back.

"Jamie! We need help! Run ahead fast and find your father. I'll come right behind with the baby."

All three of them ran for Johnny and the wagon, Jamie sprinting ahead.

Johnny was waiting for them, worry on his face.

Hazel was waiting, too. She grabbed for Charlotte. "I'll just give Charley a bath, Maggie. You'd better attend to yourself!"

Johnny dragged Maggie into the tiny caravan. He carefully shut the door and burst out laughing. Right in her face.

Maggie lost her temper. "You unfeeling, inconsiderate, tactless *male*! Johnny Stuart, this is *not* a laughing matter!" She was still jiggling up and down, unsure where to begin.

"Your tongue, Meg, your tongue! Such words do not become your womanly charms." He was still laughing, holding his sides now. "How could you do such a stupid thing to yourself?"

"You'll find out if you don't help me instantly!"

Johnny swallowed his mirth and began helping Maggie divest herself of her garments, throwing each item outside the door as soon as it was freed. Maggie was down to her skin and beginning to loose her hair when there was a discreet knock at the door. Johnny poked his head out carefully. "Yes?"

"It's just me," said Gwen. "I was boiling some water anyway for the dinner, and thought you'd need it worse right now."

Johnny took the offered bucket. "Exactly what the doctor prescribed. Thank you kindly." He firmly shut and bolted the door and returned to his wife. "Never let it be said that Johnny Stuart passed a lady in distress without offering assistance." He grabbed a cloth and began to bathe his wife's body, starting from the toes up. Maggie worked on her hair with a brush from above. They met about halfway, at waist level.

Johnny was still chuckling. "Fifty scalps have been taken. The enemy has flown in complete defeat. I believe I deserve a reward for unusual bravery on the field of battle."

Maggie laughed at last. "Oh Johnny, it was so silly of me. I was worked up over a poor little Indian baby having its head flattened. I saw nothing else, save the river upstream from which I expected Gentry and his Danites to fly into view at any second—"

They roared together like idiots. Only slowly did Maggie and Johnny sober in each other's arms, further scalp-taking forgotten.

Maggie emerged from the wagon a new woman, Johnny strutting behind her. He squinted at the bright light, pulled his shoulders back, and went off whistling.

Maggie stood sniffing the crisp autumn air about her. It was filled with the smells of cooking, and she was ravenous. Gracious, what was happening to her! She had no fire, and her family still needed to be fed!

Gwen walked over, twinkling, to inspect her friend. "I guess you didn't need the ointment Grandma Richman left on your steps, after all. Come and get some dinner.

Hazel already did for the children and the dog."

Maggie was blushing. "How wonderful to have someone else in charge for a change."

"I guess we all learned a few things about giving and sharing and growing on this journey, Maggie Stuart. My cooking may still not be up to yours, but I'm not afraid to offer it anymore."

Maggie took Gwen by the arm and impulsively gave her friend a hug. "Gwen, dear, it will taste like manna from heaven. Lead on."

twenty-one

Gentry's bateau reached the Chutes as the sun rose from the east behind, ending the foul weather of the previous day and night. They'd run through the night on purpose. Gentry knew his companions were ready to drop from fatigue, but his purpose would not allow anyone to rest. They would have all the rest they needed when the Stuart Party was within their sights.

Hoskins shouted over Gentry's shoulder through the roar of the Chutes. "Sounds like a bad one! We ought to pull over and portage!"

Gentry signaled a rough no. "They've too much lead. We'll chance it."

Hoskins's face showed confusion. Confusion changed to outright fear as the rocks and spewing water of the rapids came closer. Gentry was overdoing it. What benefit to the Mormon cause to have seven brothers drowned? Their leader's mind, however, could not be swayed. Hoskins gripped his paddle and readied himself for the plunge.

Jack Gentry helped the last battered, sodden comrade from the waters of the river and turned to study their craft which had grounded at the base of the Chutes. It could be worse. A few repairs would be necessary, but it would take on the river again. Gentry joined the men who were shivering around a small fire. It had been started on a hearth left by their recently departed prey. "They've not much of a lead on us. We'll rest and make repairs until tomorrow." The glimmer of anger and

177

distrust grew in the six pairs of eyes facing him. Gentry added casually, "We'll portage at the Dalles."

Incipient thoughts of mutiny were quelled in general relief. Gentry himself went to unload the emergency barrel of tar strapped down in the boat.

The Stuart Party's rafts left the Dalles the next morning and reached their final portage, The Cascades, that evening but had to hold up the next day because of dangerously high winds.

Finally they were on the Columbia again, drifting through a totally new world. The mountains rose majestically around them, fiercely, freshly green after the world of dun sands, sagebrush, and desert left behind. Slowly the magnificence made way for views of greater glories in the distance—the virginally pure, snow-capped cones of Mount Hood to the south, and Mount St. Helens to the north, sun glinting sharply from their icy surfaces.

Maggie sat in front of the raft now, on a long log Johnny had positioned there for this very purpose to keep them from the wet at their feet. Charlotte was in her lap. Jamie was close at hand. Hazel and her children rested next to them.

Since the incident with the fleas, Maggie had given up worrying over Gentry. Life was too short, and it wouldn't help anyway. Best to just enjoy what the moment offered. She sighed in contentment, feeling almost free again.

"It never ends. One wonder outweighs the next. Just think what it will be like, Hazel, jumping from bed each morning—every day for the rest of our lives—looking out the door and seeing those mountains before us."

Hazel pulled out a handkerchief and snuffled softly into it.

"Why, whatever is the matter?"

"They're so *different* from the hills of Pennsylvania! My mountains were sort of run down at the edges, softened like. They had a comforting look, as if telling me that my father and his father before him had helped to tame them. These mountains . . . only God could tame them!" She blew her nose.

Maggie would have put an arm around Hazel if she could have spared one. "I don't think God wants them tamed, Hazel. They show a different side of His glory . . . not stern exactly, but tall and deep, with ragged edges of power. A lot like the people come West to pass through them. We're not the same as when we started, Hazel. We're not nicely rounded anymore. We've picked up a few jagged edges." Maggie paused. "I think it's a good thing, too. We're going to need those edges to survive, to teach our children to make their way in this new country."

Hazel wiped her eyes on a sleeve. "There's something I have to say, Maggie."

Maggie dragged her eyes away from the glories around her. "What is it?"

"It's hard to express, but I mean it from my heart." She caught her breath, then let it out slowly. "Meeting you was about the best thing that happened on this journey. Besides your helping to save my life, that is. A woman needs a friend to talk to. Max promised me—just last night it was— that he'd take up his land allotment not too far from where you and Johnny get settled. Close enough so's we can visit when we feel the need."

Maggie freed up her arm now and gave Hazel that hug. "It will be a great comfort to me, too, Hazel. I've never before had proper women friends. Only my mother. We were so isolated on our farm. And when Johnny and I took to traveling after our wedding, well it was always 'here one day, gone the next.' We had time to meet a few friendly faces, but not to keep them. I'm praying now that Johnny's wanderlust will stop right there in the Willamette Valley, that we'll have a real home for ourselves and our children at last. And real friends to treasure."

Both women took in the healthy children surrounding them, the mountains and river beyond. They'd come so far, yet had managed to hold on to the most important things. Surely their remaining wish would be granted to them.

The afternoon passed as in an idyll, a dream. But by late afternoon the dream was beginning to change before their eyes. Heavy clouds had descended from nowhere, blocking out first their view of the great volcanic mountains, then the diminishing Cascade ridge itself. High winds rose and began to buffet them. The children were hustled into the safety of their wagons, and Maggie, after seeing that her own two were securely tethered inside, braved the still increasing winds to visit Johnny at the rudder.

"What's happening?" Her voice rose to challenge the sudden tempest around them.

Johnny opened his mouth but his words were blown away from him. He struggled visibly with the unwieldy rudder and tried again. "Get back to the cabin! At once! We're coming to Cape Horn. It has sudden storms like its namesake!"

Maggie fought the winds a moment longer. "Will you be safe?"

Johnny checked the rope he'd tightly drawn about his waist. "Safe as a baby!" But his grin was strained. "Get inside so I can stop worrying over you. Please!"

Maggie turned to do his bidding, then changed her mind and fought the winds to look at Johnny again. Her eyes took him in, then went beyond, to the river they'd already traversed. Between the haze coming off the water and the dark clouds lowering from above remained a short, clear space of clarity. What she saw within that space made her stomach roil.

"Johnny!"

He caught her gesture, if not her voice, and spun to look.

Gentry and the Danites had caught up with them at last. One of Fort Walla Walla's bateaux was following them, coming ever closer. Johnny almost thought he could see the look of grim determination on Gentry's face at the prow.

"Get back, Meg! To the children!"

Maggie stared one more time, then strained against the wind the few yards to their little cabin. When she reached for the door, the force of the wind almost blew it from its hinges. She struggled to pull it tightly closed again and fell into the wagon, heaving from the effort, from the sudden shock of seeing Gentry after she'd allowed her defenses to drop.

Bacon was moaning. His lament was higher-pitched than usual, almost like a keening. It could be heard above the wind. Maggie pulled herself up and stroked the coyote's fur. Finally she turned to her children.

"Mama. Papa? Mama! Cold!"

Maggie gathered Charlotte into her arms and stood by a window next to Jamie. Her son put an arm around her waist, snuggling as close as he could. They watched the scene unfolding before them in tense silence.

The wind had whipped the river into a gray froth. Coming up ahead was a new bend, with a towering cliff on its north shore. The rocks of the cliff dove straight into the river, with a force of boldness that was awesome to see. Waves dashed upon these rocks as an ocean must against its shore. Maggie had never seen an ocean, but looking, she knew.

She could also see several of their fellow rafts in front of the cliff, bravely trying to steer away from those rocks. A wrong move would mean certain disaster. The raft and all aboard would be turned into splinters in split seconds. Maggie watched as one veered entirely too close. Then she could watch no longer. She closed her eyes and prayed.

Jamie had not the same compunctions. He began to shout above the din, narrating the scene with frightened relish. "It's Grandma Richman's raft, Ma! Jube hung his old red-checked shirt up like a flag. It must be Mr. Chandler steering. Wow, it's getting awful close to those rocks. Now we're heading in toward them, too. It must be the current."

He rubbed his eyes as if disbelieving what he saw. "There's somebody hanging out of Jube's wagon! I think it's his little brother Lycurges, the one that had the putrid sore throat yesterday."

Maggie opened her eyes. She couldn't stand it any longer. Seeing *couldn't* be worse than hearing.

It was.

The Richman/Chandler raft was nearly atop the rocks. It was swaying drunkenly, undecided on its final move. A youngster in shirtsleeves and long pants was hanging suspended from the rear opening of the white-top, arms flailing, a thread of rope dangling like an umbilical cord from his middle to the wagon. Behind him, arms were tugging at the rope violently. It had gotten stuck, part of its length tangled under the wagon itself. Maggie watched the life-and-death drama, afraid to breathe, unable to offer help.

The raft swayed for another moment, suspended between the rocks and the river. Maggie could see Chandler bowed over the rudder, putting all of his considerable strength, and more, into it. She could almost smell the fear. Fear was emanating from the rocks, the river, the whirlpool. It was being blown toward their own craft.

Of an instant, a blessed wave came to lift the logs away, to send the raft out of danger, farther from the ragged rocks. The raft rushed on into the mists. Lycurges Richman was still suspended, limbs limp.

Maggie gasped for breath and slowly felt her heartbeat begin to steady itself. It wouldn't be for long. They were the next raft due for the maelstrom.

She spread her feet wider to take the added jarring of the wagon upon its logs. She hugged her children to her until it hurt. They were barreling toward the stony ledge themselves, being pulled by the crazed waters into the vortex. The last raft of the Stuart Party. But no, here came another craft.

It was Gentry's bateau!

Faster than their own, it had sped ahead between themselves and the rocks and was trying a complicated maneuver to complete a turn before them. Would it work?

No.

Their own raft was plunging with the currents toward both the bateau and the rocks. In a moment they would meet, splintering the bateau through its middle. Even Jamie shut his eyes this time. Would they make it? Would they get through the rocks, past the Cape to the final smooth waters of the river beyond? Would they ever see their promised land? Only God and Johnny's newfound strength could help them now.

A crash was followed by a shuddering crunch. Maggie's mind blanked into stillness.

twenty-two

Ten rafts limped toward the palisades of Fort Vancouver the next afternoon before sunset. The Columbia was wider here than the great Missouri and smooth as a bath—placid and calm.

Johnny threw his arms wide open to it with awe. "It's the relief after the catharsis. Just as the ancient Greeks spoke of it. We've come to the new land scourged and freshly born, by the mercy of God." There was a new reverence in the hushed tones of his voice.

Maggie stood beside him, taking one last look upstream, one last look East toward all they'd overcome. "There was no way to save any of those men, was there?"

"We've gone over it, Meg. Their boat was cleanly stove in. We'll not be hearing any more from the Danites. But in dying they gave us one final gift, albeit unwillingly. Our collision with their bateau gave us the edge we needed, the final correction to keep us off the rocks ourselves."

Maybe there was a justice to the pattern of life. If Jack Gentry hadn't pursued them, it could be her family now floating in a watery grave. Maggie gave thanks yet again, then forgot the East to turn at last to the West.

Johnny saw her final acceptance, and threw ropes to the waiting men onshore. The men had come down the smooth escarpment of green grass from the stockaded walls of the vast fort before them, ready and willing to welcome the weary pilgrims.

But Maggie's thoughts were still with the great river. It yet had a few miles to flow before it reached the sea. They were gentle, broad miles—miles which had brought the great sailing ships which stood anchored before the fort as if in a harbor. Ships that had been beyond. Beyond what the Stuart train had survived. Beyond to another world. Could this planet Earth truly go on forever? Pray God she'd never have to find out.

Their raft grounded on a soft, sandy beach with a gentle sigh of relief. It slid a few feet and stopped. Johnny guided their children and Bacon from the craft. He returned to swoop Maggie up in his arms, to carry her with aplomb to the solid land. Still in his arms, their lips met and lingered for a kiss of thanks, a kiss of promise for the years to come. Johnny eased her then to the firmness of the earth. They paused on the grass, as if in a dream.

Johnny turned to the rough woodsman who'd aided them. "Where have the ships come from, sir?"

"Them? The four-master, that'd be from around the Horn. She come in last week. We're just now loading her up with skins and lumber for the return voyage. The other come from the Sandwich Islands. It brung strange things— pineapples, coconuts, spices from the Orient." He paused and spat a thin stream of brown tobacco. "I can't think who'd be wanting to pizzen themselves on such."

"The Sandwich Islands." Johnny's eyes had a new gleam in them. "The name brings such exotic images to the mind—"

Maggie grabbed her husband and gave him a shake. "Johnny Stuart! Don't even *think* it! We have arrived!"

Johnny grinned his old grin. He watched their children scrambling past the sand, up to the green grasses of the new world. He took Maggie in his arms again in a great, exuberant bearhug. One of his old war whoops split the air, this time for sheer joy. He dropped her, breathless, next to him.

"We *have* arrived, Meg. But a man can still dream!"

A Letter To Our Readers

Dear Reader:

In order that we might better contribute to your reading enjoyment, we would appreciate your taking a few minutes to respond to the following questions. When completed, please return to the following:

Karen Carroll, Editor
Heartsong Presents
P.O. Box 719
Uhrichsville, Ohio 44683

1. Did you enjoy reading *The Promised Land*?
   ☐ Very much. I would like to see more books
      by this author!
   ☐ Moderately
      I would have enjoyed it more if _____

   _____

2. Are you a member of *Heartsong Presents*? Yes   No
   If no, where did you purchase this book? _____

   _____

3. What influenced your decision to purchase
   this book? (Circle those that apply.)

Cover	Back cover copy
Title	Friends
Publicity	Other _____

4. On a scale from 1 (poor) to 10 (superior), please rate the following elements.

___Heroine ___Plot

___Hero ___Inspirational theme

___Setting ___Secondary characters

5. What settings would you like to see covered in *Heartsong Presents* books?

_____

_____

6. What are some inspirational themes you would like to see treated in future books?_____

_____

_____

7. Would you be interested in reading other *Heartsong Presents* titles?　　　　Yes　　No

8. Please circle your age range:
   Under 18　　　　　　18-24　　　　　　25-34
   35-45　　　　　　　46-55　　　　　　Over 55

9. How many hours per week do you read? _____

Name _____

Occupation _____

Address _____

City _____ State _____ Zip _____

LOVE A GREAT LOVE STORY?

Introducing Heartsong Presents —
Your Inspirational Book Club

Heartsong Presents Christian romance reader's service will provide you with four never before published romance titles every month! In fact, your books will be mailed to you at the same time advance copies are sent to book reviewers. You'll preview each of these new and unabridged books before they are released to the general public.

These books are filled with the kind of stories you have been longing for—stories of courtship, chivalry, honor, and virtue. Strong characters and riveting plot lines will make you want to read on and on. Romance is not dead, and each of these romantic tales will remind you that Christian faith is still the vital ingredient in an intimate relationship filled with true love and honest devotion.

Sign up today to receive your first set. Send no money now. We'll bill you only $9.97 post-paid with your shipment. Then every month you'll automatically receive the latest four "hot off the press" titles for the same low post-paid price of $9.97. That's a savings of 50% off the $4.95 cover price. When you consider the exaggerated shipping charges of other book clubs, your savings are even greater!

THERE IS NO RISK—you may cancel at any time without obligation. And if you aren't completely satisfied with any selection, return it for an immediate refund.

TO JOIN, just complete the coupon below, mail it today, and get ready for hours of wholesome entertainment.

Now you can curl up, relax, and enjoy some great reading full of the warmhearted spirit of romance.